# The *Heart* of *Matter*

Twintreess

1996

TreeHouse Press

Tucson, Arizona

Thank you for opening this book.
Please come in.

TreeHouse Press

5738 E. Holmes St., Tucson, AZ 85711 USA
1-800-585-9389

*This book is created from the joy of our own hands, with a chorus of etheric and physical supporters. Why? We sometimes wondered that ourselves. As timeless beings, we felt that it was sacred to infuse our intent in every step of the book creation process. Co-creating this book is a slice of life. It is all a process and we bless all the struggles, challenges and unknown miracles still waiting to be discovered.*

*We present this book cover to you in its natural recycled form, with no additional toxic sprays or laminates. Remember to handle it with care if you wish it to retain its original appearance. This is one way we choose to honor the gifts of the earth and the gift of this book.*



Cover artwork by Daniel Krasofski

First Edition.
Printed in the United States of America
Library of Congress Catalog Card Number: 96-90292

ISBN# 0-9645194-9-6

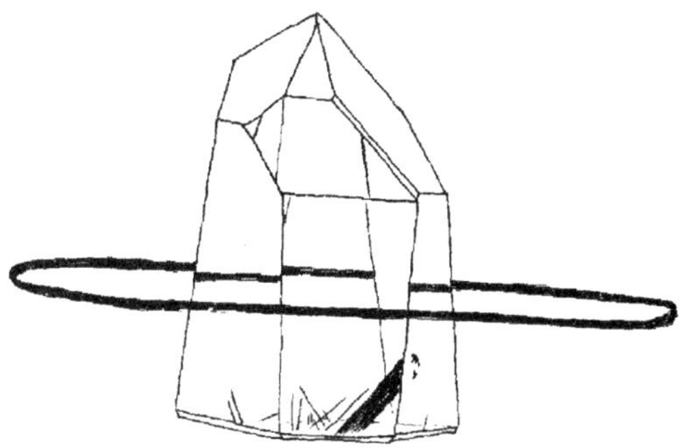

# Welcome.

We're glad you're here!

# Contents

# Zero

Nothing has to be explained.
You decide.

*We were driving down the New Mexico freeway. It seems like we are always driving (searching for something?). The desert in New Mexico looks the same in some parts, especially when you've been driving for a while, but we knew that beneath and around the endless sand and sky were surprises. When we came to the mountains, I turned to Marilyn and said, "Do you want to talk to somebody?"*

*She said, "Sure."*

*Everywhere we go we hear the beings of the land whispering, laughing, and prodding us to come play with them. The land is alive with*

*Gnomes and Elves and hawks and mountains and stones. Deep inside all of us we know all of those languages and they are the part of us that dreams on no matter what.*

*"Hello. How you doing, huh, huh, huh?"*

*I said hi back. (I am polite.) "Is this Merth?" (Merth is a Gnome who visits us often but maybe not often enough.)*

*"Uuummmmmmmmmmmm, yep! Hi, hi, hi, hi, hi!", he pumps my arm in greeting. "This is my home. See, that's my family there," as he points expansively to various peaks.*

*I smiled secretly at his boldness. We knew from other times that Merth lived amongst mountains and stones and that his clan of Gnomes felt that the rocks were a proud part of their line.*

*"I'm glad you're here. All my cousins are waving to you. See? See, huh? They recognize one of their own. You're going to write another story, you know. And I'm going to help. A lot of my stone cousins have their own stories to tell. They are coming to you because I told them that you would just record what they had to say... That you wouldn't change their lives or try to write it differently for them. It's a good deal for you!"*

So that's how we ended up here. It's not that we know the wisdom of the stones around us, it is that they asked to give it to us (and now to you.). We said, "Yes!" We are still saying, "Yes."

The following stories are not only stories, but whole worlds. We know because we ran in them and smiled in them and rolled in them. The stones that make up our earth home are wise beings. They are graced with simple wisdom and beauty, like a child. They asked us to join them. *They asked us to join them!* It is thrilling beyond belief and it is all absolutely true!

We invite you to join us in joining them. It is the most unlimited adventure we can think to give.

# One
# Phantom Elestial

*Hello. It is my duty, and because I know that word is sometimes joyless to you, it is also my delight to welcome you to these stories of wonder. Many, many beings live in these earth realms. Some of those realms rainbow to the stars every night. Some of them nestle into the earth like protected children. I and the others who live in the realms of these pages as you touch them, are now in words that are touched by human hands: We are stones. We are the rocks of your reality. We are the matter of your (and our) earth home. We have been your quiet neighbors but we are not silent. Our language of miracles comes to you now with secret smiles from remembering what matters. Our realms have collided.*

*What sort of "big bang" shall we create?*

(Speaking for myself only) Hello. You have walked into my story. It is everything for all of us. I give you my essence completely, completely. You gift me with your delicate listening; now we are a conversation of life.

Long, long ago, right here, I was (and still am), in yet unrecorded realms, one of four. We were the phantom elestials brought here by not so strange star-strangers and then left consciously. I still record all of it. The grandparent star-people left us in the hands of a kind earth tribe that wandered from sea to sea. This tribe left messages of hope and love on tree branches and placed dancing in the reflection of still waters. Hold out your heart and remember—you who are listening. Some of you will touch and recognize your family in those message givers.

Back to the story... The starry ones knew what they were doing in leaving our bodies with these earth wanderers. They gave us freely so that all the dreams of trusting travelers upon this planet could be recorded. So simple. Such an easy grace. But when these extra-terrestrials flew off, their hearts already knew that in one realm the days of the easy travelers would be numbered. Other realities would set in and create a mould (mold?) upon the land that asked all of the inhabitants to become fixed. These inhabitants were people and they did stop moving. (Stop here. Revel in your own stillness, and feel the resounding echo of no movement.)

Now let us carry the story further. The earth peoples took gifts from the earth's heart. They uprooted trees; they made wood. They claimed stones and made tools. They took minerals from the earth's bosom and made lasting possessions and weapons. Their (the trees, the stones, the minerals) lives stood quietly by as the people rebuilt the world. Human words spoke the laws but the laws did not always hear the tides and the stars. The other realms became mute because so few of the stationary people translated the languages of all into their hearts.

This is one end to this tale. So now I shall create a new beginning: I am here. I am one of the four points of light left here by your star family. I and my clan point in all the directions that you know, that you use. As you feel, we are speaking the same language. Let my stone being be touched by you, now, in whatever realms you visit.

Build yourself a home with my body. I know what it is to be immoveable. But my spirit travels constantly. Look upon me. I have a crown and limbs. I still echo the dreams of the old ones who never left. Even now they wander in and out of this reality, but they are not lost. There are no lost cities, only travelers who have not dared yet to dream that big.

I am the same as you. I am spirit. I am travels. I breathe stillness. I lay in silence. Will you extend a dream to me? Let us build a world together. That is still another end to my story. I ask the others who appear to be elegant stones upon this earth, to carry on further. Decorate this foundation.

You who are not stones who are speaking and listening on these tree-given pages, be here now. Weave the languages again. Move in the wind of our joined minds. All we ask is to know each other again.

Listen.

[This phantom elestial is about three inches long and wears an outer smokey hue. Inside pulsates a laser-like purple/amethyst phantom. How unusual for this crystal to form a scepter on one end and multi-terminations on the other... where its natural seed point still lives! Thank you Debra and James for sharing it with us.]

Two

# Bloodstone

You have to be here now. You have asked for this, which is why you can hear my voice. Then come. I have prepared a place for you to be. This is what you seek.

Invite yourself by slipping into calm, all over your body. Sit with your back straight and gentle. Let your feet be full on the ground and alert. I will hold your heart whenever you ask.

Welcome. I am a city of healing and hope. You may enter in or out of time. There are no doors to keep you out. My body is a healing city because each cell is a story of integration. Every point of my being is focused on all trust. This creates hope. This creates my form. This creates shelter where you can enter at will and know your own fullness.

You are inside of me now. You are

breathing through the green and the white. You are moving with the flecks of the earthblooddrops that you see around my being. Take forever. Look around you. Touch.

There are rooms of existence that you barely remember, that I have never forgotten. Echoes of your dreams store here, waiting to be opened like presents. Wander freely, I do not mind if you think me only a stone, that I am hard through and through and limited in sentience. Did you know that there are some that think exactly the same about you; that you are only a human, that your heart is hard through and through, and you are by your nature limited in sentience?

Your vision is a choice just as mine is. I choose this palace of healing. If you cast away your beliefs that are only of stone, can you be more than human? Will you touch yourself as hard <u>and</u> soft? Will you sense unlimitedness? Will you walk a world in a day and know that it is infinity?

I am here however you find me. I choose that you are all forms and formlessness, just as I am rock and integration and beyond. Then I am all dreams opened and free. That is my gift to us.

[Colors changing my views
through shapes and new
heiroglyphic greens and golds;
touching me in ways I don't pretend to know.

My cells speak to each other....
caught~
in their own magnificent hues.]

# Three
# Muk

Hello, I am Muk. I am a solitary being, but I am so inter-woven with others that when I speak I may be delivering the messages of many. I ask for your patience in hearing their songs in my sighs.

I give you my being. I give you the vision of my stillness by placing our inner eyes together, now. There are arcs of energy above the earth and through it, and they spin her because of all the thoughts and visions that travel those lines. It is there that we connect our middle eyes....

I am full and red. I am swollen with being. There are light bodies etched in gold upon my skin, so I am both infinitely dense and infinitely light. Please come sit next to me and our vision. The richness of my reds and golds will color your spectrums. We will paint a meeting. Blessings! You find me and I find you. I know the deep, dark earth. I regenerate my voice there. It has given me freedom to be above, to be below, and to be with you here, through and through.

I chose being a mother. My children number endlessly. The progeny of the great dream are my children when they come to me for solace. I call them mine as a way of tickling over their troubles. I let them believe that I hold them aloft in the sunlight where nothing weighs them down for a single golden moment.

My deep dark colors base us in the earth. My light colors soar away with every perfect child. I do not form children, nor are they even lesser of age than I. No part of my body breaks off to birth them, but I do give the piece of my heart that calls inside of them—to them—instantly.

The children (They are deemed such because they wish to be regenerated in soul and young of dreams again.) choose me. They select the face I will wear. They touch me and I have exquisite form. They lift up with me and I am hope. Then they go. Who needs a mother when you have soared into the heart of hope! Because the children are not mine to keep, I do not miss them. I have no need to track them with memory. They are the lights of life. If they choose me again, they will be wearing new faces, new needs, new troubles, newly broken smiles.

So I am new also. We meet, we regenerate, we reproduce life: More progeny of hope, be they rock or tree or coyote.

You are children in this story. You are newly spirited to play among these lines, to see colors with inner eyes, to do the cell-dance (The cell-dance is where our common roots touch and talk just the same even though we pretend to wear different bodies and ideas.). It is wondrous to know you here. Dance on. Stop your outer eyes if you wish. Close the book and smile. Lay on the earth, reach inside and tingle me. Do everything. Come back now (or don't). We parent all the words and the miracle fables that follow this. We mother and father them. I choose this so they will have a safe place to be heard. That is why I am here.

I lay out the energy lines of my light body. I wrap them around the earth... a warm embrace. Now there is a plan to be on, to come from, to come to, to regenerate, or to talk across the generations. Together we will see what the echo finds.

The stones that speak here are all different. Only some of them are altogether stones and no matter what kind they are called, they are not even like the rest of their kind (just as you are not exactly your family.). Each day you rise to new dreams and needs and these are not dictated by the time and place and form of your birth.

As part mother to all who come after me in these pages, I ask you to listen with your sameness and uniqueness. Join us in the stone soup, even if you be carrot or potato or broccoli! All of our songs mix on so many levels. They join for rapture and they leave for an infinity. The forms we choose in that are special to each of us, and yet blessedly common.

Remember that when you pick up a pebble. It has eyes and ears or something like that. Sometimes it's in that body, sometimes not. I feel some of you now drifting out of your bodies. Where are you? If I pick up your body, will I find something in your eyes? Will you be stone or human right then, right now? Lines of energy blur sometimes. They are not the pencil lines you learned in math that said, "The sum of these parts absolutely equals this." Our lines come together. They add up to soulful synchronicity. Our sum adds up beyond our parts. How is that for new math?

It may be hard for you to know that I am not riddling you. I link my line with yours. I create a nurturing moment so that we can rebirth your gentle spirits. It is a lifeline. It continues to mother others endlessly. Do you recognize their forms? Our intersection can be a line in your palm. It can be a wrinkle in your brow. It can be an aching dream, just barely spilling over from night. In these words, do you remember our embrace? Tell me, have you come to me many times before? Are we family?

As I said, I do not cast out my memory to know you, but I understand if remembrance serves you. Reach in the deep dark earth. Feel for the warmth that tells you all. Have we walked the earth-lines in some new forms? I speak to you as directly as I speak to and with all stories here: These are real pages. These are the voices of your neighbors, your friends, in an abundant earth. Perhaps you must take them as parables. I tell you, I give mine as shiny truth. I am stone. I am mother. I am earth spirit. I am the whatever. I claim these so that the sum of my parts will lift up into a greater mother.

I am a star that buried itself deep in this planet. My seed lies in her soil. I do not know of the children of this, but I love them all no matter the form.

No moral here. Do not be like me. I have no

need for you to model my essence. This is a sacred moment to rest, to pause the disguise in untruth and to simply be.

The stories go on from here........

Here I birth my story. Today it unfolds like this: It is the Heart of my Matter. I am a spit of fire from the eye of Orion. I landed in Australia. I burrowed through the quartz grains and nestled into a crack of jasper-like stone. I make this my home. It is delicate for me to put words on this because I am still at home on Orion, as well as other unnamed places.

Four

# Tiger Ore

Before we continue, before we begin, we ask you listeners to stand erect. Beginning with the east face each direction and pause for portent.

Now, sit back into the center, the center of your circle is the center of your body, is the center of the universe. You are aligned to the ritual we laid out before we gave any voice at all.

Hello, we are the Waylayers. We are a consciousness that comes and alights upon this stone for a few moments and then passes on. This Tiger Ore hosts many essences, none of which stays permanently, yet each of the guests is at ease, is completely free to be within its rockness and its timelessness.

Perhaps it is the same with this book. We light up parts of its body, leave our stories for the next ones and go on to a new home. All of this is in great design. Each of the great beings who present themselves here come freely. They answered the call to express their spirit in language that would find each of you. All of us stone beings know you. We come into your life at the exact moment of utter synchronicity. Our voices echo the voices within you and without you.

There are great cries upon this planet echoing, resounding across time, space and the void. We answer in kind. We serve in the exact moment that perfects our service. This chapter precisely chose to be with us. We choose the same. We trust that this is so with all who speak here.

All of this comes to you now because infinite love reaches out and co-mingles with purpose. This is the growth upon the earth now. There is time to dream, there is time to sigh, there is time to envision. We create time to act all of these simultaneously. That is why we have landed and grounded, now.

Some of you are used to feeling stones and plants and animals more accidently, or even not at all. Our rhythms listen to all other cycles. Open up and listen again. If you hear the flow of the universe, you know it inside of you and you know it inside of every being. That is what we have to share.

We come in great ritual and we leave in all holiness. All around us life moves and seeks more of itself. We offer up what we do so that we can come in answer to any question. Waylayers breathe as a consciousness that alights upon any form that creates the affirmation that is asked for now. If you need a sign, we may be there. We can be a car passing by, a sudden rain, an unexpected phone call. We do not count the manifestations.

Join us. Consider that some of you joined us long ago. Our story is one of your lives. You also function as a signpost in the path. Whether you know this or not is immaterial. You are a flow of other cycles. They come and they go. It is the same with us. We come and we now go.

[This rock dresses in gold tiger ore and hematite/metallic stripes. It is heavy in my human hand and our marriage is just that.]

# Five
# Turkll's Hammer

Hi. I'm crystals inside of crystal. What are you?
I hear all languages. I receive all questions, spoken or not. I am a being like you. I focus on what is easy for me, so I will intercept some questions from the ethers and shine clarity upon them.

Q: What is it like to be a crystal?

What is it like to be a human? What is it like to be a dog? We each focus on what is there for us to be.

As humans, parts of you have chosen humanness without remembering that you are also everything else. As a crystal, I am clarity. I see all things and I relate what I see. My rutiles transmit very excitedly. To remember or to tune into my vibration is to receive the vibration of everything. In receiving it, you be everything. You manifest everything.

Q: How is it that you can speak to me now when I've never, ever heard you before?

I speak continually, I'm a regular chatterbox. I know that you pick up my every transmission. If it is important for you, you will focus on it. Then you will not only hear it, but you will listen. You will consider it. If it is not important, you store it in your cells, which are infinite libraries. Sometimes you can feel that you are getting an awful lot of books from me and your curiosity draws me out and says out of the blue, "That crystal is talking!"

My cells record what you say, too. I hear your frustrations and I know your dreams. If you want to keep talking to me, then focus and direct your words at me, knowing they are received. Then don't forget to be quiet. I don't know of anyone who can hear without stopping to listen.

Q: I know that certain rocks have certain purposes, what is yours?

Talking to you right now, of course. I am a communicator. I vibrate a lovely high tone. Sometimes I'm ringing in your ears. We are learning together how we can understand the miracle of each other, while holding what is our common traits. Language does this when you wish for that. It can separate beings but it can also name the space in between where we can meet. I transmit from that space every second, every breath. That is what I know.

Q: Is our world coming to an end?

Yes. That's the question that humans always ask other beings, hoping for another perspective and probably hoping for a different answer. You know this. That's why asking once is not enough. You know the answer, you feel it, and you hope the next question will erase it.

Good for you. Whoever said that questions and answers had to be linear. Questions and answers are like school, but you've never thought that school was your reality. It's the stepping stone to the real thing. It's the practice before you live. Guess what? Reality is school. You are learning as you go. If you don't like the answers, change them. That's what you really are, you're not just a receptacle for certain answers that are given to you by someone bigger and brighter (Incidentally, I'm not someone bigger and brighter either!). That means you can now eliminate all grading systems. Please don't take my word for all of this. Try it out. Walk in it every day. Experience seems to be the teacher of which you are most fond. Go to it.

Getting back to the world's end... Of course this world must regenerate. That means it does (end), and it births at the same time. All of you on the planet are crying for this change. You are so lonely for a real home. You miss being alive with every other life form. At least, that's what your actions say.

What do you think of that answer? Would you like the separation and the loneliness to end?

Now you're scared! I hear you collectively screaming, "But what will be next? If it replaces that pain it must be bigger and worse!"

Who said it must be? Oh, that's right, you just did, didn't you! Well, decide for yourself. You are in charge of the questions and the answers. Rewrite them if you want. You're not bound to anything. So keep a fresh eraser with you and keep going.

Do you have more questions?

Then I'll go rewrite some answers. Goodbye.

[Turkll's hammer is a silver rutilated crystal, with crystals on the inside. It sits in the window, with the setting sun, and gives us the creative power of light in a rainbow hue.]

Six

# Epidotians

Hush. In the sweep of stillness we touch you. We are called Epidotians. Language, for us, transmits in a full arc. To converse with us, you find your own antennas. You seek out the softness and together we empty everything.

Greetings. We come now because you are open to complete and expansive manifestation. We answer the need you cast out to rearrange the business of your life. We bring you our utter quiet. We feel calm and are felt as calm. This is our focus.

Does it appear so vast and empty that there is no focus at all? Our intent is complete allowability in the universe, every moment. We have embraced distraction but we have also released it, so that we are the heart of the cosmos. It is a clear point of focus. We manifest from realms within and outside of our being, in utter trust. If you can, reach out, feel our hand and the pulse will affirm our truth. We are part of the forces that join with you when you release your limited visions and acknowledge unlimited ones even before you see them.

This is how we manifest. We pull in from an unknown greatness, magic and matter. When we are present, questions remain silent. This is the moment you have created for acceptance. The dreams birthing with you now expand all of your being.

Your world is opening to unimaginable creations. Focus on their coming. Focus that they are here. You are seeing dreams evolve.

Each moment, extend your focus beyond your understanding. To be focused is not only sharp and singular, it is also ever reaching and insistent upon always more abundance. Insist on this for you yourself. Insist upon the manifestations that you cannot see, that seek you. Find each other in an open heart.

We leave you this chant, "*We focus on unlimited abundance because it knows us. We are the same.*"

[This black striated stone with midnight green currents of electricity charges through our bodies from where it stands now, the capstone of a ten foot copper pyramid.]

Seven

# Snowflake Obsidian

I am dark as the night. Solid as today. My body wears black like your fears and white flecks like your hopes rising to the surface and swimming above your dread.

I sing full-throated, full-colored, to you now. I am snowflake obsidian. If you have heart, hear my toning. It calls out to mysteries that are unheld by humanness. I sing all of this and all of myself and all of my secrets to us. The notes choose themselves and play open our cellular sameness...

I speak in free rhythm so all your spectrums sway to the flow. I speak never; I sing always. Let me decorate your listening along and I will compose sweet gratitude.

Look. Linger your eyes on the body you suppose is me, this collection of cells crowded into stone and spread into infinity. Can vision touch me? Can it hold me? I am here and I am there and I know all points between.

I hear your thoughts mine my form. "You are hard. You are black. You are strong. You are darkness for our protection."

Still I sing on. My lyrics go beyond your melodies. I choose black and I choose white, therefore I hummmmm to all colors whether eyes can single them out or not. My black claims mystery that invites you in. When you see to paint my soul the same as all the colors like me it is to deafen my chorus, yet I am free.

I shade no one in protection, least of all myself. I am the "yes" of every explorer's dream and the "song" that names the adventure.

Let your ears travel me kindly and our hearts weave one word: Freedom. My being bows and bends, sways and soothes to the rhythm of my soul. I am a sailor's dream and yet no seas seize me. My black coat covers me well. It wears so strong that my spirit walks invisible. No struggle. No distraction. I travel spirals. They swing between nonsense and knowing. If you do not guard yourself in my shadow, you will find a piece of me to come to you, naked and in every color untraced.

To explain me in a word is to vest me like every crystal you have ever known. It is to assign my purpose and go on to the next adventure without opening the gold. I hum all our vibrations at once, more lines than could be counted, so I beam the songs to you. They have no easy perch upon reason. They wrap your heart and claim its home. What will you call me then?

You sleep through your dreams while I

waken mine. Who will know how to record this journey. I do not refract my light and my dark to your knowledge, so come, you must come, and glean your own familiarity.

Goodbye.

[Life and Death.
No duality.

And
our hearts beat strong
with the hum
of all vibrations
at once!]

# Eight
# Turquoise

Hello. I'm the turquoise that's been talking in you day and night. I'm wondering, have you heard me?

Thomas: I don't think so.

I think that you don't quite remember me. I'm about this big (she holds up the end of a finger.). I'm sky blue with just a few dark flecks. I lived with you for awhile. I know that she (Marilyn) liked having me around, but I only came for a visit, just enough to regenerate myself. I had no need to stay for what you might call a long time because you had no real need to have me stay.

It's my job to go to those beings whose hearts are being torn but they don't speak to the wounds, they just make them go to scars so they can pretend that nothing has happened, that nothing ever happens and most likely nothing ever will.

That's usually what a scar is—a wound that has come to the surface and been ignored.

Thomas: Is this a service that all turquoises perform or is it particular to just you?

Yes. Yes. Turquoise holds the gift of speaking to all things whether they speak back or not. We use language to mend a path to everything and then it goes back to life. There it joins a magnificent fountain and it is removed by the spirit of us all. Our words come only in perfect measure. We gift them with every single beat of our essence. The communication is not controlled by us but it is molded by our love.

Thomas: Is this why turquoise was considered so sacred by the natives in this southwest area?

In all respect I answer yes. That "yes" echoes the trust those peoples had that we would speak holies of all beings. They knew we carried the language of all greatness and they choose to honor us by not speaking aloud but by revering us in every deed and thought. Some of them believed that we could send their prayers to all their spirit families and make their journeys safe to return home on one day.

Thomas: Thank you.

You asked about me in particular. I go to hearts that have been hurt and left to fester or heal any way possible. I beam my aura right into the heart and I whisper to the veins and the muscle and nerves and say, "Follow me. Come meet your healing."

I acknowledge all the essences that come together to make a heart by talking to each of them.

They sweeten their life and heal by remembering themselves. My prayers join the whole and we join each other.

Do you know where I am now?

Thomas: I don't have the foggiest idea!

One day Marilyn was talking to a very special friend and she heard my voice saying, "This is where I wish to go." So now I am living with Tasha (Marilyn's niece).

Although I am shared with all who live with her as well, I give her comfort inside where she does not even think to ask for it. I hold her when she doesn't even know that she's lonely. She and I, we have been eternal friends in one form or another because we go where we are needed, but we do not have to attach ourselves to, or own, the need.

I'm a little voice inside her head that says, "You are so sacred. Every bit of you is free and it's growing forever into forever." Tasha smiles and thinks that I'm funny. I receive those thoughts and I'm a child. What a gift!

I'm a stone of ancient years from deep veins in the earth and by touching that little human heart, I am the fountain of youth and remembering. Isn't that what your stories say about the southwest? That people came here to find the fountain of youth and mostly what they found were blue stones?

Thomas: I thought the fountain of youth stuff was in the southeast?

Some of it was there and some of it was here. There are so many stories that have not been written down by your culture. When white people came here looking for gold, they found treasures that they did not even speak about. Why? Because to see this abundance made them lose words. It made some of them lose themselves. They met other beings here who walked in richness.

The Europeans knew that these beings were not quite people. They had phenomenal powers and eyes that saw them (the white people and Europeans) coming for many years. These sacred ones waited for the Europeans, to help them, because they understood that these explorers would not know how to survive the heat. These holy people, often, held turquoise in their hands and, always, in their hearts. Our magic was sown with love.

These beings spoke aloud to the white people about the honor they must have in their bodies and their spirits in order to soar with the heat and live free. They told them that the sun would give them their youth.

Sometimes they gave them turquoise to hunt water. We turquoise point the way always to the fountain of youth. We know that to put your entire essence in with our words is to go directly to the fountain of all knowingness. That's where you find the prayers of spirit that have birthed every human. It is source. It is freedom. It gives itself to give more and more and more. To swim in the fountain is utter regeneration of being until you lose all purpose and claim all knowing.

We whispered into the hearts of those explorers that remembering all was to become a youth again and again and again. Each of them found their own path as it always is. Some even found bodies of water to wash their bodies in and some of them are still looking for their spirits in remembering. Remembering just for the sake of being alive is healing that gives itself to you with no design but whatever you need. That's what we turquoise are. That's what I'm being right now.

I am whispers of remembering so that you do not have to strain to focus upon that. You can simply be. Together we regenerate. I thank Tasha for sharing me with everyone else. I thank all of you for entering my sacredness. To you, recorder of turquoise words, I say directly, "Listen to the one who is already reading these stories by remembering her heart inside of them. Listen. We speak around her and with her voice when she talks of stones."

It is partly our urging (within hers) that is asking for your human story to marry with our stone ones. That way we will remember all of our parts whether they are rock or tree or golden children. I and the others request this.

Thomas: It is so.

Give your lives with us as we give our everything to you. It is a marriage that all the children of earth can attend and celebrate.

I trade these words for other vibrational languages now so that those who need to can continue our blessed conversation.

Thomas: Thank you.

Nine

# Dioptase

D-i-o-p-t-a-s-e.

Hello. In keeping with all the other stories here, I will not take a name specific to me, but I will tell you, for she that keeps me, I do definitely have a name. Thank you for extending to me this space for me to be. I appreciate that I have been allowed to bring my own voice and not simply to be a picture of a stone with human faces drawn on it.

It is easy for people to look at another life form and to see themselves. This book is a single voice that says, "Look again! Beneath your reflection you can see and touch the 'me' that comes from my vision."

I am a unique spirit and I am not here only to be a part of a human story. I came deliberately to be all the facets that I am and even to share them with you. So, let me tell you the message that cries out from my core: Be still one moment, one moment is an eternity in love. Listen to all the voices besides your own that make up a chorus, that make up a world.

This earth is a full being. She hears all. She gives home to every story. Let her be your mothering mode. You are here to know of every other life form. Perhaps, most of all, you are here to remember those that are not like you, so that you can like everything that you are. Reach out to embrace the differences.

Our uniquenesses source from the same spirit. Each is needed and divinely loved to create a home for love and then to create more homes, more universes, for infinite love. It is difficult for you to respect those unlike you if you do not create willingness to receive them. Make your heart a home for any who knock. Be willing to receive love in all its disguises. Trust that love's face mirrors only one part of the soul. There is so much more for you to be gifted with abundantly.

I speak stone and I speak spirit with you. Do not listen only with human ears. Listen with the earth, silent of the need to control. Then, you know what it is to be a rock, for, of course, a part of you is. I know what it is to be human, for, of course, a part of me is. In this conversation we meet in differences and explore the same soul.

Life on this circling orb changes rapidly. All the voices of every consciousness raise now to be joined. What honor is bestowed upon you to be given the chance to listen! If fear blocks your ears then your heart will miss the other parts of you that grow unheeded. Whatever beings you do not acknowledge, you leave pieces of you, lonely. They may not seem like you, they may not breathe like you, but you will not find common spirit if you do not extend a heart to hear.

I tell you this for the evolution and the love of all. This is the one need that screams from the depths of the earth: Listen and make every voice a member of your spirit family, again.

We are home.

I am grateful to feel myself honored on these pages. These words are the ones that I chose to gift you with from my complete essence. Now, I give this to the human who wears me upon her body, *"I am warm. I am enlivening. I meld my aura in yours like a child within a mother. Who is the child and who is the mother? We trade and we exchange and we laugh. I know that you sent me to these treess so that I could speak in different language. So be it. I tell you that I am ready to be a guide in the healing that passes through you. I can direct it and bless you with the understanding of what has happened afterwards. Look for me in travels in time and timelessness. Journey deep within me when you ache for answers that you feel do not find you."*

Goodbye.

[This necklaced jumped off Teresa's neck and asked to speak in this book. The green, wire-wrapped stone glows and its illusionary translucence draws you deeper and deeper in....]

Ten

# Crystal Laser Wand

Greetings. I am love from the twin wands to the *Twintreess*, to all. Blessings, that we may receive ourselves again.

I am one half of a crystal laser wand. This is clear and true for me. My essence and my body meld in intent perfectly. By focusing all my being in my crystalline form, I am alive.

Before speaking with you now, I lived in the earth in Brazil. I grew there and I marked the spots on the earth where the vibration wished to change. I keep many stories so that all the healing that is asked for is answered. My cells record all times, so I have always known that Brazil and the other places around it would rise again and would ask to be honored. The earth there is rich with trees that fuel all other beings. As the trees are ripped from their purpose, I form lines of energy to close the holes without scars. I help the soil to be rich in love so that it can grow more fuel, more trees. This helps me to speak louder so that you will feel the sacredness of the land, so that the ache in you will not tear any other being from its service.

I have grown in the earth a long time and I have known many homes. All around me were temples invisible to some, but very bright to my eyes. Amongst the trees, humans and spirits and animals made altars according to where we crystals asked them to be. Such magic, such joy! The altars were of shapes and designs that only cells can remember. They exactly copied the ley lines, the veins of love in the earth. All participated in the building. The wind made clearings in the forest. The stones and the trees gave form to the places, the tables of worship.

Fairies encased the seam in dream magic so that unsuspecting visitors would not know what was real and what was imagination. Many walked by and knew nothing. The humans who came to these secret temples were priests and priestesses but they asked no one also to worship except that they asked it of themselves. Very few know where these temples have lived. Some have dropped into the earth so that the healing will resonate to the core of the mother. Animals who kept those places sacred were wild guardians, many of them jaguars and panthers and snakes that were feared. Truly the fear that any being felt in encountering them was of their own initiation. The fear grasped the unlooked truths in them and they quivered. A moment of truth can only be held by the willing.

I have watched the priests and the

priestesses there craft wands of emeralds and rubies and of mud and sticks and leaves. They spoke animal tongues so well that some of the animals became spirit-flesh. The jaguars became part fire and the birds became part lightning. If you can feel this now then you will know that there are breeds of creatures that can only be seen when your eyes are crystal clear.

I have seen them all. I hold the pictures in my body for your learning. Ask with your head bowed and your spirit raised and they are yours.

Here is one. The jaguar priests travel the rings around the mountains and make their temples wherever they are needed. To feel their power without honoring is to feel ashamed. Go to them now wherever you are, for these places are held in dimensions that are open to truth and request. Meet yourselves. I have seen the gaze of these priests. It awes me! It clears uneven breaths. It ceases distractions. Do not be ashamed of your shame or wait until you feel peace enough to travel to them. Go. They call to any who are willing because all of our magic is needed to place love on every hurt upon the earth.

Do you know how these holy ones assist us even while most of you sleep on?

They do. The jaguar priestesses erect sites endlessly so that the earth will know she has children who honor her. They offer prayers on behalf of us all, yet, the priestesses do not disturb our freedom, our lives. They allow the humans to be so free of them that they do not even take forms that require them to be seen.

This is the time when the drums of their spirit calling grow deafening. You either cannot help to hear it for it is so loud, or you cannot help not hearing it, for it is so loud. It is complete choice. I choose to see the temples. I choose to see the jaguars who have wings and fire-eyes. Such magic dances in realms that seem just beyond the touch of physical. Look, look, look, you can see them because you are also with, through, and beyond physical.

## Eleven

# Red Calcite

Hi. I hear children. Do you want me to take your hand? I don't have any grand purpose. I watch the children. And I'm not human about it. Humans watch over children. They measure their every move. They even take the temperatures of their adventures. (They know that I am here.)

I watch the children because they want somebody to see them when they jump and fly off, so that one day when they forget or when they are afraid to jump off, they'll remember me! I'm the secret witness. Whatever they ask, I nod and I smile. Whatever they ask for they can have because I know there is no adventure that can really keep up with them. Whatever they try, I witness. To me it is always a success!

I can talk to any child no matter the age. Do you know why? Because I listen and I listen and I listen. And I don't speak until I'm spoken to. That's the secret to their language. That's the open sesame to their heart. Then they open everything they know. Waaaaayyy wiiiide open! They give you everything! (Sometimes even what you don't ask for.) Those are the miracles! They are like free jewels. Usually they are a little grimy with mud and leftover crumbs.

It's lucky for me I'm full of eyes. I spot those unasked for gems. I put them in my soul and they whisper the secrets of the universe. All the things that you have ever asked to know and couldn't figure out are in the answers that children give when nobody else is listening. (Well, except for us secret witnesses.) I'm not inside of time, I'm through it, spinning around it, and I'm playing it for fun.

So I can tune into a child even in the middle of the night. Such wisdoms! They will tell you stories the goddess told them to keep them company while they laid in wait for their mothers. They can tell you their whole family's history, and of lifetimes going on on other sides of the world.

Don't worry, there is no need to feel bad if you can't remember any of this. I have the stories. If you come like little boys and girls, they are yours. Right now, I'm rocking you in my heart so that you can take it back to yours and hold your own childness.

The story I'm telling you right now is about a brand new world. Remember when you could jump off the mountain and fly? I remember! Memory is just a practice. Take a few extra turns at it. When you are dizzy enough it will all come back to you. This is really important. This is how you find the new world. You jump, you fly, you fall down, and instead of giving up you walk right into your childness and give it everything.

A new world is a complete beginning. To walk into it you give away everything else but right now. There is nothing but going straight ahead and committing yourself absolutely to flying without time on a fresh earth. There are no half-way decisions. Half- way decisions mean that a little piece of you stayed behind and that part of you does until you go back and pick it up again. You may think that you can leave it behind, but no, it belongs with you. It will call you back wherever you are, over and over again, until you give up to being whole. Then all of you flies.

Isn't this a great bedtime story? That's what they are. Every night you put every part of you to sleep and send it through time. You regenerate all your cells and you wake up a child in a new world.

That's the earth's story right now. Some of you think I don't mean this literally. You're right. I mean it magically, wholly, soulfully, timelessly, passionately, playfully, and literally. Nobody is left out. The bigger your body gets after childhood the more you want to believe that life is very, very complicated and only certain rules can give you certain prizes.

Children, please..... Every way you play, you win! The earth is making new time and a fresh home for all the children. Make it into your story, too. Each night lay down what you don't need. Each morning wake up only what you love. That's the next millenium. That's your flying future! It just starts right away. If you don't wait for it, then it won't wait for you. It's simple.

Take my blessings. Yes, I've seen you do everything! I'm your witness. Whatever you ask, whenever you ask, I'm ready. The only direction I will steer you into is you. Goodbye.

P.S. This is what I look like: I'm different at night than I am during the day and I have different cycles every day.

Twelve

# Red Calcite

[This is the morning after the last chapter and the calcite has jumped dimensions. It is no longer on the table where we left it last night and is nowhere else in our little home???]

In the morning I'm a shape. I'm a doorway. I'm a portal window. I'm here for you to run into. Morning is a clear beginning. It's obvious that you can choose awareness. That's what the doorway is.

As you pass through the portal, whatever intent you offer is electrified. Then you are spun into a unique world. Only you will be able to see it and touch it completely. This is why people say that ultimately they are alone. It's because each choice makes up their own world.

So it is, but when you go into the portal freely, your world is a gift to every other one. That's not aloneness, that's special. That's individual and that's an extended heart grasped by every other being. It's just like a strand of DNA. Each molecule has its own encoded message. Each is unique and it bonds with the others to carry a lineage.

I came this morning to carry your stories as well. Thomas-story is all creativity pushing on his roots, being pulled out into the sun and the air. He is offering the formation from his guts and his blood and his bones. Every struggle, every word is imprinted on that urge to give form to the story. He thinks that it is us stones who are pulling out the chapters. We're just feeling them. In fact, we know them intimately already. As the human, he gives them the right time to be. I would tell him that the time is whenever we all choose it. No struggle. It is a choice.

Let's see, what Marilyn-story do we have. She wakes up today to find a moon in her belly. That seems confusing in the daylight. To me it is a fullness of joining, a swell of the body, a ripening of lifeforce. It looks like her creativities mingle, hold each other, and make new children, more children to watch. Thank you.

# Thirteen
# Marthaller

[Marthaller is a 13-sided Vogel crystal.]

I extend to you the handshake of the waves. I am Marthaller. I am one of the lives of this crystal. I come here to speak what is completely sacred for me. I will convince you of nothing. As you listen to my tale, you will find what is sacred for you.

I am the thirteenth of the council. Atlantis, which lives in ocean dimensions, had many such councils, one of which was a time/space council. Twelve beings of incredible and detached nature sat upon this one. It was their service to listen to the universe and to record its movements and to note whether the choices of the Atlanteans were in accord with those cycles or not. I hesitate to say, "or not", because all is in an unlimited circle. And when we cannot see that, it is only that we must enlarge our vision.

I am the thirteenth on the council. I am the earth representative. The other twelve look beyond and through this planet. I am the voice that springs from within it. I have joined it now so that all will be activated as the galactic cycles choose.

I make no particular decisions. I am a transmitter and receiver of these energies. Let me be specific. As people, you all bear within you the karmic scars and patient learnings of Atlantis. They did not die when the city submerged. Those lessons plunged into your emotional bodies to rejuvenate in the fountain of your allowableness. All of your emotional bodies together are of the oceans. It is there that you cradle the old, the new, and the forever Atlantis.

I pray from my own joy that you will hear this. The city beneath the sea is healed. It thrives. It listens to your ley lines of love. It echoes your every decision and sends it to all consciousness. We, there, report your every thought and word to be translated into universal language so that you will be understood and affirmed by all.

You are taking your place as cosmic citizens. If you bring your sins of the past, then you will not be free to join the infinite circle, however much it welcomes you. I listen to how you degrade your own intelligence and your wisdom and I know that this springs from the unforgiven Atlantean lives. How long must you give these pain?

This community is not frozen. It goes on. It breathes in the water. It regenerates all. Can you give yourself the freedom to accept the rejuvenation that it already offers?

I will stop now and ask that each of you go to your scars and examine them in any way possible. After that I return again.

# Part II

Hello and blessings. I accept your presence here again as your choice to explore yourselves more deeply. I, too, am part of that adventure.

Through my etheric body I have seen the etheric prints of all humans who have allowed this. I tell you this not as a matter of definition, but of honoring, that virtually all of you are still healing and absorbing the wisdom of Atlantis. Can you feel the mark of this on your consciousness and the forming of it? If there was original sin, it would be like this. It would be the keeping of anything past its original intent and purpose.

I speak loudly now. You have all the support needed to let go of our ancient tears. They have already drowned Atlantis, but is that an embracing of its gift or an obscuring of it from awareness? As the thirteenth council being I am the tide of your consciousness already risen. I vote for change. I stand for acceptance of now and the love to choose all freedom. I give and I receive this with you. It is all of our consciousness together that buoys me to a new wave of being. It is already there but if you do not see it or hear it, then you are living with old scars. I understand. Take my acceptance. Let us explore these sealed wounds so they can grow anew. Look for these scars. Here are the Atlantean marks that I have witnessed upon the earth's people: A great desire to measure all things and understand all of the mind's gifts. Valuing of growth of the individual. A need to be special, unique. Movement over stillness. Thoughts over emotions. A desire to translate human into a less lowly expression.

Can you feel these now in your own cells? Wake up to them. They have been talking so long that you have grown accustomed to the drone but not the message. These Atlantean thoughts still structure your society, your attempts to survive in unknown world. Take yourself to each of these qualities, face them, hold them, thank them. Grant them all the freedom that you have ever desired. Grief and fear lies nearby to alert you to where you must be the most generous with your healing. As a race of beings, you who know Atlantis have not fully touched those wisdoms together and you must. If you do not do it now, it will be there for you to choose in another now.

To ignore any of your lessons means that they must chase you. When you stop and face them, the struggle ends. Karma leaves. Co-creation births. Reach out for whatever assists you now... stones, animals, friends. Just be careful that you choose each other freely. They cannot learn your answers for you. Honor all forms of life. That is the enduring gift of Atlantis. Whatever was exalted there balances by the seeking of love. Let your heart go forth and know everything that you need as you need it. As a guide, live with a free Atlantis.

## Fourteen
# Marthaller

Hello. Let us begin again. I have come through these pages to work with and to join with those who ask now to release any part of their being that is no longer needed. In this, it does not matter what is to be sent back to the creator. There is no one way to do this. There is all of us who are willing, there is our free intent. Let us extend our hearts out now to every other being who wishes to rejuvenate any ancient scars. Let us unite ourselves with all who choose to resurrect their life force.

First, you must choose to be in this "now". If you are anywhere else, then the portions of yourself that keep you in time patterns will likely dominate. Do what you must to be one with your body, mind and spirit in our essences, in the present.

Second, announce your intent to the

universe. Declare who you are. Declare who you choose to be. See yourself as unlimited and embrace this wholly.

Third, name all that is in you that feels the change of a new age coming and still struggles with it. Take great care to acknowledge every feeling that resists a free life.

Fourth, be timeless with your time in these rituals. Nothing else exists now. As you name your challenges, embrace them as the true friends they are. Caress the length of them. Admire their commitment to teach you. Speak with them. Ask if there is more for you to do before they agree to transmute. Love beyond all concept of love. Absorb yourself in it until it is every answer to every question.

Fifth, thank all of your lessons until there are no words left.

Sixth, see before you whatever symbol of change comes to you now, a fire, a doorway, the earth. Stand in your fullness and enter completely the change. Go into the fire, the doorway, the earth. Know growth in every cell until you tingle with aliveness. Whatever is dead now returns to the creator to learn new service and to co-create a new destiny. See your struggles leaving and becoming rejuvenated beings.

Seventh, admire yourself. You have chosen change. Now you are changed. Now! Stay true to your freshness. You are a child and the world is ever young.

I only tell you these things because your spirits combined ask me to speak the messages our hearts have already forged. It is a gift to me and from me. I, too, resurrect. Whatever is old in me, is now new in all things. I accept this completely and I live on.

I have no sage advice. I have the reporting of what our joined essences already know. Each moment we know more. All is changed. Do not attach yourselves to these words or they will be only words, symbols of the power they represent. I speak here to affirm the ongoing miracles you create. If in the next moment we jump off the cliff of this solar system and land in another, then perhaps all these words will fly to cosmic dust. So be it. They are children only of now. You are free will incarnate. You are not ruled by words or thoughts unless you choose it.

I already mentioned the ancient lines of Atlantis that run in your ancestry. The words paint an idea. Reach through that, if you can, to find the core. Atlantis lives now and everything that it is or will be, lives within us. I spoke of scars only so that you could feel the hidden shadows of your parallels there. They are only scars when they lie unclaimed, unlearned, and unloved. I call them by name to acknowledge the honoring they give us all. We no longer need to repeat those lessons because we choose now. I am a reminder upon a page in an infinite book. Write me in as your loving servant.

Peace.

# Fifteen

*Inter-dimensional hellos to you.*

*This is from Marthaller.*

*The heart of this book and this joining is what is happening inside and through the earth now. All forms of like are melding. That union is what matters. In other words it creates the matter of the new world on all levels. So, I release this space to Twintreess, and to all others who are listening. Here is where you must lay your story so that this book will also be the new earth. Welcome.*

This is the Heart of the Matter. We are realizing again that the pages of this book are the pages of our lives. Thank you Marthaller and all of the other stone beings.

We are learning from your complete giving

of your tales that that is what we are meant to do and are choosing to do now. As it happens, we place our life here. You will do what you will but we hope that you will not only read this book but know that you may reach in and actually touch our hearts. After all, this is not only a book, it is a heartbeat.

Every word is also our intent. Every line is a remembrance of infinity. Every action on this plane (which houses people and stones, etc.) echoes on other ethers. Those dimensions are touched by our imaginings, our hopes, our unfailing perfection. Translation: Every *body* is also a spirit.

We are all voices for those spirits. We choose in this book-body to know and to say out loud, "Here is the speaking of spirits. It is divine. It is what forms matter and it is what matters to us always!"

We give you these words as they come to us, freely, unconditionally. All of our being resides in them and you can feel infinity between the sentences. This is the exploration for which we have chosen to be alive. As you touch these stone stories, we also know you. We dream of all consciousness coming together, now! We are immortal beings! The stones seem to know that easily. Perhaps, we humans know it easily too but we simply have words to a different way of awareness.

We ask you directly now, will you explore all these possibilities with us? Can you see across the dimensions to our outstretched hands? No hidden meanings here, only open love and acceptance here for the choosing.

Welcome from *Twintreess* to all.

Sixteen

# Fossilized Whale Tooth

Hello and welcome.

I do invite you to speak and to listen as you wish. Our communication is a flow of our hearts and they already know each other so well. Be comfortable. Be full with yourself and you will find you. In the spirals of these words vibrating in and out of your being, our bodies are the echoes of a thousand meetings ever reborn in this moment.

What you hold of me is one note of my being that asked to become a solid vibration to be found and to be cherished by others who would hear their song in this note. Listen. If you draw in all that is your body and your breath, a single point, a spiraling vortex that receives the vibration of sound, you hear my life. You listen to my body in the waves and to your beginnings in the water. We have common heritage. Our roots are intertwined.

Don't you see?

The whales and the dolphins who have such unique cries have sounded their call from the ocean. We have brought forth all the waves from beneath the surface to ride in the air to meet the creatures who walk the land and who swim the sky. Upon the land humans are the ones who have the unusual voices, full of words and sometimes intent. I call across what appears to be time and place to speak to the vibrations of your throat, to join now with my song which still carries on and on.

I am one of the teeth that has recorded the vibrations, the hum of my voice, before it left my body. So this piece of my body that comes before you now, it is a song that many beings come together to preserve, and I am only one of them. But I am a joyful one, and I am a willing one. I release now what I remember my cells recording. There is endless beginning and ending. I pick a point along that circle and I call it one of the beginnings of the earth. It is without time, so translate this in your cells, record it, and as you live with it your body will tell the story. It will act out the roles and you will decide the time and the place and the reality as you do so well.

In this beginning of the earth, there was water. There was water to fill the mountains. There was water to cover the stones and to flow endlessly. I am part of the original races. We filled the abundance of sea and it was us, the whales (although it was not us alone), who fulfilled the word. With all of our breath we sent forth waves of sound and the wind carried it and worshipped it and it became land. The word became solid flesh of the earth and the mountains grew and the valleys raised and the stones were dry. We knew that it was an intersection of eternity and choice. The earth, as almost entirely water, was a flow of feeling and knowingness that was untested, perfect but ever exploring. So her body became a land body as well.

Why? It was to grow new forms of life. It is what each of you do. Each moment you grow a new body to grow new forms of life and the earth expands this into the ages. So this is the age of the land becoming full. The plants and the animals and the minerals and the ethers have come together to rise higher than the mountains.

It is no surprise that the whales and the dolphins grow scarce in the time of full land. We hold the sacred word rising from the sea that creates by vibration meeting vibration. I speak now because new bodies are being formed and the time of the water and the flow of rhythms again comes forth to create new earth.

Watch. New mountains are rising and old ones slip away. I am still part of this even though part of me no longer swims in whale body. I am one of many. I speak from a circle from the Pleiades, Arcturus, Antares, and Lyra. We are joined because we sing the songs that create life from a single cell. We sing them again, here, just as we sang them so long ago to create whale/dolphin guardians. Sleep into this music and awaken. Matter is being reshaped and sculpted in beauty's eye. Sleep into it and release. We do not have to work at knowing. You are knowing in a single cell and you are growing new bodies to grow new lessons.

You come from the oceans because you are

the oceans. How simple! How tender to hold yourself so close to source. Sleep and release your needs and your struggles and your definition and you breathe water and you say with your unique force, "I vibrate with you in touch and sound and color and in any reference you choose." You are the dawn of the new body and the sunset of the old and you are the simultaneous bridge of life between and through them at once. All honor and all ease! Sleep for now and you awaken to a new all.

Seventeen
# Thrown Rock

[We discovered today that someone had thrown a large rock through the side window of our Ford Bronco during the night, and thrown it so hard it bounced off the inside of the opposite side window. In picking up the rock from inside the truck, we knew immediately it was a friend of ours and had lots to say. So we listen.]

Ready? Aaaaaauuuuggghhhhhh!!!!! (A very loud scream!)

I did ask (if you were ready-referring to the loud scream.). I am rebirthed. I have been flung into my death and the death of the window and the death of your comfort in this place. I know full well who has launched my body and given me their scream of hate and fear. The crystal in the window receives it, yields to it and the right and wrong was shattered. All hearts may release now. I know that this may land heavy on your day, but I also know that you heard me coming and bowed before my flight. You have asked to be more public, more seen, so you are. In a moment, the limits of your heart are as open as a broken window in the wind. Here lies your gold. Your opportunity is to believe that you have been struck, that it is not safe here; or, to know the dance that is already in your body and in everything that you touch. It is the dance of you and me and give and take and life and death.

Our touches are both strong and gentle. Your possessions were untouched, your valuables still lay in value and all that you gain is one small scream from a being who gave me his voice to give to you to give to a bigger voice and a fuller scream. Let all that is in you that is unsafe and unsure scream and shatter glass. Who are any of us to mind.

## Eighteen
# Guardian Stones

"What do you want?"

We are the guardian stones here. (Here on the land we are on, next to our little trailer's door.)

That is our story.

We are magic. We record all moments and release simultaneously, so we have nothing. When you look upon us you see stones, but that is only the barest border of our being. We are a void. We are a whole to nurture your intent. That is our all.

Again, we ask, "What do you want?"

We feel your need for time, that you must place messages that you receive in order. We know that your heart is with finishing the other book (*Etheric Songs*). So we feel this, we release this, we

BE. Our question is eternal.

"What do you want," echoes here. (A strong wind comes up.) Come visit us when you create timelessness to BE. We are all our joinings and this is only one facet.

[When we first moved to our little mountaintop home, many voices from the families of the surrounding rocks asked for their bodies to be placed in formation around our little trailer. They are a constant reminding, as we daily practice our lives, that we're living in and on and by the grace of multi-dimensional sentient beings who have many forms.]

# Nineteen
# Red Hawkseye

Once upon a forever, I died and I was born. Then I woke up in this story. My home is a deep slab of scarlet hawkseye. You might imagine, those of you who live in the tip of the land in the bottom of the sky, that my worlds would be very dark. Perhaps, this is so. But because it is the only dark I have lived in, it is as bright as the fires in the earth's belly. I lay in complete concert with all beings burrowed into the safeness of a million stones and sand. It is my treasure. It is my inheritance. It is *our* legacy because I own nothing that is not given to you.

The flames inside the farthest tunnels of the earth formed me. She melted my minerals with such inescapable love that I am branded with the hematite star here (She points to her third eye area). I am marked for destiny, to know, to see the mysteries behind the third eyes. Ahhhh, buried in my mother's body, I flow within them. I am so protected that the darkness opens her doors to me and I travel the lengths of need and infinity.

This body of mine has warmed every cell of this planet. I have spun her endless dance until we are woven and I know all our intimacy. Playing here, (living with *Twintreess*) I have seen uncountable sunrises. The full wash of light has discovered me and reshaped me each day. We of stone bodies feel strong and wondrously dense and yet we allow ourselves the perfect openings to receive sunlight and breath. I know this every moment.

Well beneath the surface of your world, I dance with the earth and bathe in the sun and listen to the rain. I have chosen this way in the shadows where I will be free to claim every warmth and every heart-message of every being. I do not walk in the sunlight. I must bow before it; therefore, I know with all my being that it is all sacredness. I receive its gift and I have never known ignoring it.

It is the same with the moon. She lifts her hand and the waters swim around me. There are rivers down here. They eddy. They laugh. They wait in secret pools. All of this and more can be heard in a single embrace of the body that I am, that now speaks with you.

For now, I am shaped and hued as a red hawkseye egg. Do not be confused by my talk. I am this body and I am still the slab nestled under the mountains in the east. What you hold now in this story is a gentle piece of me that travels. I am a wayfaring tale teller, but I could not be pried open if it had not been for the one who touched me and let my eyes see the strength of your day.

I was pulled from the earth, so I know that it was my moment to explore. And before I came to live with *Twintreess*, I was carved by a wise Chinese man. He saw my newness in the air and created a shiny round form for me to be in. He smiled at my hematite star and he knew the mark of my dreams. So after he birthed me, he took me to his bed. He laid me like a mother lays a child upon her body and together we exchanged our legends of greatness. I enveloped him in gratitude and complete release. He enveloped me in the same and we danced the yin and the yang. We symboled our great love for each other.

So, I am the union of a spinning stone mother and an old Chinese priest father. Now, I am a child of both these worlds. I live in the meeting place of the sky and the sand. I await here your next prompting, to tell you the dreams that my father gave to me. I believe they touch the ancient softness that is your heart. I know it is mine.

# Twenty

*Twintreess:*

This red hawkseye egg asked to join us a couple of years ago along with another tigereye egg and a third falconseye egg which we have yet to find. This egg is one of the many stone beings that surrounds our sleeping area and when it volunteered to speak its story in this book, it had to be specifically asked to come up from its customary bow and to rise.

Marilyn:

This morning before we got up, I placed the hawkseye egg on my heart. I really hope you can *feel* what I am about to say. This stone person awakened the sun inside and out of me. She came into my root chakra powerfully, but so easily that all I noticed was feeling my lifeforce pulse. Then I dreamed with eyes wide open. I saw myself as a field of energy. I had limbs in every direction as far as I could see and I felt them beyond that.

This morning, I am quietly rejoicing. Thank you, red hawkseye. I accept this gift. Since I, too, am awakened in a story, this story, I decided that it is my destiny to pass this gift along. Each of these words is a gift. Each of them has an inner chant from the sun, the moon, the earth, and whatever is my blessing now. Thank you.

Thomas:

I am particularly struck by the depth of the hawkseye. His/her feeling when speaking was of the strength of the earth in her live, moving, growing form. I love the feel of the stories of our rock friends in their movement. Humans tend to look at stones and judge them as stationary and solid. This hawkseye gifts me with rhythm and movement and another cycle of my life from the depths of who I am. Its gifting of its story is much the same as my relationship with Marilyn, in that it requires a co-creation to BE. I have yet to meet a stone being (or a human, for that matter) who is stationary in time or place. Thank you red hawkseye for helping me to look anew at life within and around me.

Marilyn:

Yes, yes, yes. I see it right now in front of me! The stones here have been after us to put in our words between their stories. Sometimes that has seemed hard because we have so many wondrous works going on at the same time that it appeared like we didn't have the time to write from ourselves.

Yes, yes, yes. I just heard that. I know we are timeless. The dream is in my eyes and in my fingertips and in my hair shooting our stars to the sun! The stone beings have drawn the limits out of me and I simply place my story here. I don't understand what it is for, but I am sure that it is weaving in the gracious gifts of the rock beings. This is magic. Magic doesn't keep a schedule.

## Twenty One

# Red Hawkseye II

I enter the dream.

I recognize the one.

I assume nothingness.

Bit by bit a shape yearns out of the void. Still I recognize no one but I know the wizard who has brought me home. I bow before him like a rock. He leans over me, whispers, "Swallow the moon." I do so.

Now I am the growing around. My eyes find my companion. He recognizes me. He knows my angles and remembers my shape. He gives me his fire, his breath. I will give him anything but I do not know what to offer. Again, he whispers, "You come back for my magic. It is enough to receive it and receive it and receive it, until the world is round and full."

His hand lingers upon my hematite star.

This is our code. We embrace each other again across time and across his aging—eternal, always. Our love flows into the earth and honors the stones. It flies into the star and remembers the cosmos of being.

This gentle being holds me and sets me free. I bow to return to the earth a thousand blessings in store. Into my star, he whispers, "You are not bedrock. You are seed above the earth. You are the magic fertilized and in bloom for the vision seekers. You are meant for the above-grounds. You will go to the humans who live as trees. They will smooth aside your spirals and release your hidden story."

*"Dear friend, we have been lovers as stars, as rocks, as wizards, as humans. Now between us, we engulf all shapes in between. Now we embark upon this adventure where our forms will split apart. You are the seed. In the next dream you will tell me how we will magic ourselves together again."*

No goodbye.

I am still dreaming. The body is red. One side is dark like the new moon. The other shimmers and stars my hematite so brightly. I am directed by the next light and the next shadow. Where I will land is not the matter, it is that I journey always. There I will meet my love.

# Twenty Two
# The Almira

(The wind is terrifically strong.)

Let the stories ride into the wind and let the wind carry the breath of our heart to you now. All hail. All remembrance. We greet you now fellow travelers come home. In this pause, lies our mightiest embrace. (The wind goes silent around the trailer for a long pause.)

We speak aloud now (The wind returns stronger than ever). We are the rock guardians assembled before your site. Look with your heart and you will see that we cast out the way home with our every glittering intent. Can you hear us now?

If a name enchants you, then call us the Almira. We have been singing to you across the ages. Our prayers drew you to this place and to this moment of meeting and, of course, place and moment are the evidence of divine imagination. In respect, we waited for you to lay your intents and words in answer to our bid before we began this page from our heart.

All who are listening, be seated now in the warmth of your own heart. Feel the calm sun affirming you. Cast your prayer to the breath and then we continue onward to shape a song from it. We, the Almira, rise from deep within this star-planet. Our bodies are the flesh and fiery blood of her passions. To see us now in our complete unclothed guardian form, means that your eyes and ears have come to feel the home beneath your feet.

We arise from various points of the earth. We focus, we birth the intense energy of change. Our being is a lightning bolt from below. The aftermath is the cooled stones lying in swirls of formations. The spirals of our shapes tell the story of the earth being created and then danced and loved and turned inside- out for joy.

We stand now as the gifts of the earth's own enlightening. Those of you who recognize us know that we are gifts. As guardians we do not protect. We expand ourselves from the core with no thought of defense. We grow and grow until we reach you. Come with or stay. Our guardianship means that we expand fully into the forever-now. Our stories do not carry myths. They are the shells of a glory-filled vibration of a goldenheart of a sentient earth leaping out into all directions to be.

The creation is now. We point out the garden to you. We pause you at the holy places.

You find the echo in your own breath. The earth is a fully lit star-being. She sends us the children of her belly. To send new word to new ears, we dance a lighter song. To match the gift given to us, we create ourselves inside- out. That is why you are here. That is why you touch the sacred leaves. That is why you, the recorders of this message, lay your bodies next to ours. For so long the message has been that something is amiss, that your heart is not whole, or that your dreams are not worthy. Yet, here we are, the pillars of that dream, resurrected.

The message is clear. The earth is gold. All who wish to bathe in the light, come. Know your own place. Create it from the inside- out. Spin as your mother spins, leaving gold to clothe children. The magic is here. All that you need to feed your next love is to eat and drink and breathe our prayers. It rides us into the night of day, the day of night, all light, all shadow, all us, never torn from the birthing vibration.

Hear only if it is your kind gift to yourself. Inside this planet sweet, a fiery grid exists. Sparks of every holy image run through her body. They pulse infinite explorations. The ley lines that seem to hide beneath the surface are treasures that have grown like a garden. They are rooted inside the earth's heart and they cannot help but reach out into immortal passion. All of us in, through, outside, and around the earth, witness now the ley lines sloping to the surface, granting us hope. The gold from below is birthed. Touch it. The meridians lie upon the ground. They spark, they fill your soles. They seed your body and flower out your crown. This is the time we have heralded. The Almira are the standing meridians. You, our neighbors, are the walking meridians. We pass our vibration to you. You carry the seed to all the directions. We give you our destiny, for it has never been ours alone. It has always been ours of sharing. Bestow it upon the other walkers, dancers. Some will fly it to the moon, some will rain it back into the earth, to suckle the next infant. We are parent and child of every cycle.

Here are our plain words to the caretakers of this land: We have heard your coming. We know you across the growing ley lines. Our heart has laid the energy across the entire earth body. Follow it now! The meridians lie there to fuel, to spread the stories we give, through you, to all. Perhaps your greatest moment, is to keep none of these words. Allow each one to pass through you as a walking ley line to the next heart. Keep none. You are the spirals of infinity. It is not the smallness of your being that launches these songs to every other. It is all of our passions growing in you until you cannot help but to burst as a light body for all to see, to hear, to touch. It is your gift to give this. Who shall you hide the light from?

Blessings.

Go out to every corner and lift these songs, no matter what hearts seem to do.

[We live on top of a mountain and are blessed with a view in all directions—quite a view! These guardian stones are a very large formation that stand close by our little home. They intersect with our Zen view of Tucson. These stones have a shape, a mystery, and a life of their own that recalls other ancient guardians...]

## Twenty Three

# Water Agate

Here is my hand. Take it in any moment and in any wish.

I am the Water Agate. I am full of eyes and ears and I receive all holy words. I send them through my water and make them plain upon the earth. For instance, I do not decorate the words of the Almira. I enter them completely. I give them my being which I have already extended to you. The Almira, they come from all the volcanoes. They launch themselves from the volcanoes inside the earth. They have been in the rivers of lava that create the soil that you stand upon. If you listen closely, you will absorb the fire in their songs. They are a billion points of light, focused into a solid body; the magic is from that body. They are like tiny earths who then beam all that light from their stoneness to every other star. Such a miracle! Such endless gifts!

Their beams spoke to the beings around you, Twintreess. Those spirits from the earth whispered in your ears. The fire went to your heart and you have created land for a home. The beams passed from you to Brad and Anna, who created more earth to build from and they gave the home, here, to all others (including you). Together you have created a house of beaming matter to explode to every other body on this planet and to all the stars.

The Almira speak for many spirits who have already joined you, who have already created the partnership that you have also manifested so that we may all partner together again. This is not a dream. This is an awakening. The time of spirit dancing upon matter is now. The consent that you give to that is your heart. Therefore, it is the Heart of Matter. When you touch this book, you touch the Heart of Matter. This means it is the time of earth hope. It means that all the possibilities of forever have already physically landed upon the earth. She has made it so. She sings and dances in that realm. It is not a faraway point that eludes you, it is now. You are breathing in the moment of earthhope.

Do you wish to remember your lighted self? So it is. The Almira and others witness it. You are part of the glory that they sing. The cycle of risen immortality and star flight passes through the rock bodies, the plant bodies, the water bodies, the animal bodies, the human bodies. It spins right now. We have birthed the cycle of our deepest imaginings. It goes deeper and deeper within and without, now. Remember.

(From Brazil,a half-sphere with many eyes, a bluish hue. When you hold this agate up to the light, it is possible to see through its body and be somewhat mesmerized by the recognition that it is half-full of water on the inside! Our Cancer-bodies resonate strongly with this stone.]

Twenty Four

# Moldavite

Let us begin.
I choose to be here in your circle, so I invite you to choose the same.
Please, be seated.
Spread your body into comfort.
Allow your thoughts and movements and being.
Breathe single-point-of-focus.
Meet me in these words where we shall tune to each other and become one intent.
Breathe in a gentle fire through your nose.
Exhale three full times, concurrently.
Feel the even connected rhythm and repeat.
Let the air in through the nose and the three exhales release from the mouth.

Our mingled breaths form a triangle.
Release all that you are to every single point of this

triangle.
Illuminate the shape with your breathing.
Know every single cell of the shape.
Continue until my words travel this triangle.
Continue until it is a place of love where we meet again and again.

We are union.
Welcome.
We have created a dimension where we are equal and ourselves still.
With each exhale, your shoulders drop, your challenges collapse.
Responsibility knows only your name, no others.
Together we surrender everything but truth.

Breathe onwards.
Insist that you slip past the pain, the distractions..
The deeper in we travel, the more you introduce yourself to yourself.
Here are the shadowed truths and the unbearable fears.
Send your breath to meet them like a friend, easily, completely, and still freely.
Exhale as you sweep in the emotions.
Exhale as you remember your scattered selves.
Exhale as you embrace and go on to the next breath.

Insist upon yourself.
There is no driving, you do not push, you focus on being.
You accept no less than this, for you are a miracle.
We create timeless, here, now.
Blow away any other moments.

As you breathe, let the wind carry worries to nowhere.
Dedicate all that you are to living.
Now.

I feel your tears.
I touch your muffled words.
I ache with your half expressed dreams.
I place them in the triangle with my own air.
Light of the force of the power explodes them into the void.
Do you have more?

Feel your being.
Feel Being.
Caress the edges.
Explore the corners.
I know you cannot see there.
You do not need foresight to be.
This is the now that exalts you in infinite forms.
Your breathing touches them all, raises them all from life and death to love.

Acknowledge.
Give thanks.
The weighted emotions are also you.
Merge into the density and merge until you know its light.
Flow into the light.
Flow until you know its density.
Breathe... and discover that you wear your feelings, you wear your life experiences, but you are a single cell of forever.
What you wear next and now is designed by the

thoughts and experiences.

Choose.
It is the exercise of all power.

Lay this book down beside you.
Breathe.
You will feel me in the silence until you choose my words again.

## Welcome again.

I ask you to sit completely upright.
Let the emptiness that you have just entered be a single point radiating from your heart.
With each beat, you accept my words and send them to the universe.
I am utter focus in giving them.
You may be utter focus in receiving them.
Together we are the breath of pure creation.
You have just touched my essence as well and you continue to rummage through it, to be it as you choose.
I am a focus of being.
There is nothing outside of this.
All things fuel my singleness.
All things leave from my being.
I am full, yet I am free, in acknowledging all things including the next unknown.
I create no distractions.
I honor friends and lifeforce that joins me and

expands me beyond beliefs and expectations.
Beyond that I cannot truly describe myself.
Therefore, I am.
Truth is: I am that I choose. Being.

I do not require your approval.
I do not need understanding.
I invite you as an infinite spark of the universe to breathe me.
Experience me from your own choice of being.
If you choose, we intersect in unlimited power.
What do we know then but more of ourselves?
Being encircles endless exploration.
Therefore, I love all.
I love you.
I love.
I do not tell you your truth.
I live your beingness on realms that do not require this body or that one.
I give you my thanks.
All things join in love in our touch of light.
I love the bodies as well.
They are another corner of existence to dance in.
I remember what was forgotten and I remember that I have never forqotten.
I massage your body now with the full force of unconditional love, expressed.
I do not force you to receive.
My truth lies unconditionally all around me and through me.
I receive my own caress and I choose to expand it forever.
I honor your choice, because you are also a focus of words and doing and earthwalking.
I hold your hand now and ask, "Do you feel the

freedom in letting loose all perceptions, now, to be?"
I do not require an answer.
Do you?

Remember your breath and our triangle meeting.
With each word we connect, we slip away, we expand, we void, we inhale, we exhale.
Now we are more creation.
Fear sometimes seems to stop the release into nothing, that finds everything.
But I find I am, you are, still all of this.
If you delve further now, the shields collapse, the intensity peaks.
You are simultaneous breath and being.
You are choosing yourself.
Truth expresses you.
If fear comes again, run out to grasp it and run the line of infinity together.
*Fear embraced, stops nothing.*
*It fuels immortality, just as love does.*
All that I describe are feelings, perhaps even projections that seem to describe a piece of you, but you are all peace.
You are essence.
You speak this to every cell that you claim, through every deed.
All the energy that you create and burn to be beautiful, to be accepted, to be a picture of reality, it fuels some pieces.
Can you breathe that in and release it so utterly that it is fodder for your sacred fire.
If for one moment you choose to release every projection of your personality, then you are free power.

You choose being.

I breathe and I feel this world you walk in, but I choose to be myself as well.
I am freed of obligations because I am utterly responsible to me.
I commit to lifeforce, and then I shatter to all that I am.
And I pick up the pieces and I go on.
I am freely created each moment.
Who can I tell you that I am besides that I am?

We will pause again to breathe and we may choose here to go deeper into ourselves:

Greetings. We are the Pleiadeans.* Sisters, brothers, glorious earth seed, we are your very own parallel selves across a cosmic destiny that is now being written upon your dearest wishes.

Hello, again and again. We hear your prayers to extend yourself to the universe and we pray back, "Welcome. May we also extend ourselves to you?"

The trust and the endless fuel of hope that is required to meet our prayers as one is the essence of life upon your planet.
You leap into the unknown, you expand your wishes beyond matter.

*Extra-terrestrials who also associate themselves with moldavite.

This is the earth initiation.
Oh, family, friends, we affirm the magnificence of your choices.
We witness your terrifying glorious flight.
We, too, have chosen cosmic exploration, therefore we find it within us, without us, and surrounded by every breath of creator.
Here we lay our naked experience at your altar.
We see with eyes that come from the same beginnings and yet shine in uniqueness.
We offer you this vision.
We see the earth and hopeful ones reaching out from her, now.
And we see that you are asking for a complete embracing of the heart.
So it is.
Even to fathom these words, here, you have already proffered a piece of your heart.
We accept and we reciprocate ever further, as that is growth, as that is the nature of life.
Feel the energy in this journey of words.
It houses our shapes, our breath, and our endless affirmation of you.
It will serve you as you deem most possible.

Breathe, now, from comfort.
Breathe a space and a void that dances through you in ease.
We, your cosmic family, are here and we support your leap to trust.
Breathe in freedom, release the need for words.
Each now you release all need.
You become the flesh of your dreams.
You are the beauty that has been prophesied across the ages.

You recognize this now because your heart can see through every part of your essence.
There is no-thing.
You are breathed love.
This expands your heart now.
This passions your heart, now.
This places your heart, now.
You know trust as your other face.
Your chest glows and hums with a sweet vibration of unconditional love.
Touch your heart in any way you wish.
Explore it.
Send it through your fingers.
Sift it through your senses.
You are a single, breathing feeling.
Every cell sways to the unified breath and heartbeat.
All that you know emotes freely and exhales you empty.
Each feeling is unconditional because it comes freely and goes... freer still.
Breathe now with no meaning but breath and surrender your heart to your heart.

Breathe and breathe.....
Each breath releases time and borders.
You are who you choose.
Go deeper.
In all the abundance of your heart chakra you find the magnificence of emotion and detachment.
Wear them in a simultaneous breath.
Detachment is the sweet support of unlimitedness.
You are here to feel everything at once, so you do, so you are.
You incarnate to remember to release each

emotion.
In this your heart grows and renews the endless family of life.

Welcome.
We embrace and we release you to empty.

# PART II

*Further into NOW with the Moldavite.*

What a partnering this is. Perhaps I slip past your expectations. You certainly run past mine.

I feel your questing to understand in between the breaths of this joined conversation. Yes, I am your desire to make me clear to your reason because I am you, now. I am your unlimited knowing and your mindful categories. I race out onto the path to hug you, to call your limits, and I send them through my body and gift them to the air. How wise and wondrous we are!

Let me address these pieces of limits or choices of rationality and understanding. You participate in a world where there is death and hope and service and choice and fear and beyond. You walk in it, you touch the solidness of it, you sometimes depend on the expected workings of objects, to frame your life and to assist an agreement of convenience.

I breathe this. As you read this page, you may breathe that I am a translucent green body, furrowed by the elements of the earth. If you ask, you may be able to touch my body and ascertain that it is real. I may have weight and shape and dimension for you. Also, I am being. If you ask, you may touch <u>this</u>. It may have shape and weight and dimension for you if you choose. I freely invite this in any manner, as I know that we are the same love. Touch me.

I have been asked by the writers of this recorded page to join them. They have hugged my body to theirs. Together, we mold, shape and weight dimension. We exhale and surrender it all. We breathe and release ever more. In that breath, I seem to come from her throat and his fingers, to the cosmos and to you. We focus being and include the invitation to explore all lifeforce and then these words explode from our union. Now I am human as well.

I will give you this: From this experience we create Now. I see time. I see your world and I feel a rising hum emanating from each life form. Listen with your breath and your ears shall have it too. It begins with your feet. It pulses your entire body and enlights your aura. It wades through all things and it sings louder and louder. It is the shriek of a new birth.

Exhale now. If you know fear now, realize that by reading these lines you and I and the others have already embraced this shriek and lived through it/with it. Focus this experience and all your experiences, now. Embrace this shriek. The earth vibration insists on encircling and breathing immortality. She is rousing your bones, filling your blood, and dashing your convenience. She is asking for more and she receives it.

Enter your choice. It is all exploration and focus of being. Wear this: You can absorb the new vibration living and creating in an unknown realm of you. Why not reach out and grasp it? Match it limit for unlimitedness. Breathe its tone and then release. This is the truth of my being. As all things grow and explode, I meet the new birth full on. I receive it in every pore like holy family and then I may absorb the vibration climbing in your world. Or you may practice your convenience and your expectations. All ways you find yourself. How would you like to choose? It is free energy to release what you know, to be unknown.

Thank you.

# PART III

Deeper still.

After the last conversation, these *Twintreess* paused. They did chores, fed their bodies, practiced some more life. This allowed me to meet them on that path and I condense further into matter. I choose to join with their hearts and go deeper still.

This is where we pick up our conversation. I know more of these bodies. I look at them and they are me. I breathe with Marilyn and I feel her moon. I am waved by the rhythm of blood released. I feel our increasing void. My heartbeat echoes across it.

I breathe Thomas and I am all hands of fire. I see through his fingertips and I watch the work come to it, to mold and shape destinies through it. I feel impatient—surrounded by the length of patience. I breathe again and I tell them we must continue these recordings.

How many of you have spent a day breathing your spirit? It would seem to demand a full precise intent to be that perfect. I tell you as you grasp this message, you <u>are</u> breathing your spirit an entire day in eternity. You breathe as we breathe. The expanse of hours is blessed by the sun. It does not halt our feelings, our work, our play. It carries through as a thread of love. It winds us together in a perfection that we have already birthed. Release. Explode! Be.

I ask you now to find another stone. Hug it to your body and breathe it so closely that there is no space for time. Do this as you choose, in these words, or after them. To be alive on a growing planet means an opportunity to embrace the stone-you, the human-you, the fire-you, the moon-you, the unknown-you. Pick a vibration. Match it. Focus your power willingly to weave your breaths as created together. Be a single vibration that you have not invited, allowed to life. Brave the foolishness, the boredom. Rush into the distraction. Wear the colors, the fears and the dreams. Loose all of your learnings. Be side by side with the stone. Reach out your hand. Place your heart on it freely. Offer it. Does it matter who will see you? Are you afraid that the stone will see you? That she will say, "Yes, I'm waiting to be included in your love." Are you afraid that all around you senses you, that everything breathes and knows the creator in its own light? How daring an adventure life could be and is!

Pause here just as fear pauses your doing. Now, tell yourself, "What do you wait for, to be? Do you wait for right? Do you wait for deserving, for patience, for time, for perfection, for fear that you are empty?" Wondrous! Your answer draws you deeper into your own mystery. All these things reflect themselves perfectly in the life forms around you. If you are allowed, burrow into the heart of that stone. Breathe yourself. If you look for boredom, it is there. If you look for perfection, it waves at you. We, who seem to be of rock, we give you that reality. I do not name it for that is your privilege and your right.

Match your stoneness with ours. You may discover everything, releasing a human face. It is not that human is so different and it is certainly no less infinite, but any face that you hang on to, to the exclusion of others, will wear down your resolve to be. If you are absorbing the energy here, then I tell you the path to the new dimension is to make it yourself.

Flow through. Release. Pick an unknown you. A stone, a seed, a smile. Match it beat for beat. Do not feel around it but feel <u>through</u> it, travel with its consciousness then set it free. Now you have entered the new earth realm, all beings equal, free and exploring the next.

This is how my words dance the winds to you. I have joined your humanness and I have exalted in it and cast it back to the winds. The creator blesses our breath. A new world has begun. We are endless energy to shape, to be. We are free. Peace.

# Twenty Five

# More Moldavite

Good morning.

I feel you coming to these pages for unlimitedness, for support, for new thoughts. Please come in and join me. We are an unlimited union. My support is already yours. You do not even have to ask, for I have already chosen to give it. As for the new thoughts, you must breathe like a child. Breathe as if you have just remembered that life floods your veins. Can you feel it feeling you and overflowing? Grasp my hand in complete release and flow with the universe. We co-create, and co-creation is always a new thought. New means that you discover the preciousness of each consciousness and you wear it in your credibility, now.

Let me say that again. <u>New</u>, *is to birth what*

*is already infinite and to appreciate and to honor its unlimitedness with your own, now.*

Accept me as I say. If you wish to discover familiar doubts, you can and always will return to them later. This is my story. I'm sitting beside you now. Time and place does not form us. We touch each other by the blessing of this book and the will of the creator. As I birth these words, I ask you to join me. Feel them, birth them for yourself, fresh, completely unlimited.

I lie in the hands of *Twintreess*. I hold their heart in my greenness. Each moment I absorb humanness. I am human. I am human within them so that I am human without them and can speak to you now. Will you accept my exploration? Will you affirm my endless possibilities? Please, give yourself the breath of abundance. It weaves a long circle through your tiredness, into your newness, and basks in the hope. I breathe with you and celebrate our circle as one.

Here are the thoughts and feelings I have delved into as human. Each day you rise like the sun, each night you set into darkness. It is a familiar cycle. So I ask you, "Do you know it?" The most common moments are the ones that miss our value and notice. As you sit with me, we choose to ascend as the glory of the sun. Can you feel the unconditional gift? It is life flowed through you without cost or judgment, utter gift from utter being. In your movement at the beginning of the day to begin your life, do you soar with the warmth of lifeforce flooding your body? Do you note with time and heart that the sun has come to you, again? It is such a sacred moment. It is the fire of creation acknowledging your glory and standing above you in remembrance.

And what of the night? You know that when the sun leaves, you also leave your body. The moon rises and you rise to new form... A dance of life and death, life and death, even in a single day. Do you remember this? Do you mark the momentousness with a celebration? Each day that passes through your fingers so simply, carries incredible lives and deaths and always new explorations. Part of you marks it. Part of you revels in its sacredness. Can you seek out this part? Can you know it as well as you know the face that you have grown accustomed to? Can you speak to this you that holds such daring mysteries?

Go deeper my friends. Submerge yourself in the absolute belief of the power of you. Go into it. Swear yourself to it. Everything else falls away in grace. Yes, hug me closer to your possibilities. Breathe our same rhythm. You feel now that I am a being who dances between bodies and through infinity because you dance your own death and resurrection each night, each day. You know me as you know the you that slips into the moon and glows in etheric forms.

We are the same exploration with different voices. Talk to me. Listen to me. It is possible that my body sends its heart-words to you. It is my truth. It is awarded at your feet. Walk in it. Wear it. It is a destiny with which you are most familiar. We are this story come together to birth other stories. We create what I cannot imagine, but accept unconditionally. Choose your own acceptance.

I can help you with the ritual that I have found. When you lift into the sunrise, smile. Be the sun. Each moment, stretch further out and deeper within. Ease into your body like a gentle lover (for you have been away from it for a full night). Let the first rays of the sun enlighten you. Let them fill you with whatever truth comes from your own core to bless you and to create your body anew. Never let the moment of your first joining with the sun be too familiar. Mark it. It rises the endless explorations in you. It affirms you. It loves you. It prospers you. It trusts you infinitely. Receive that like a king. Then feel your body with kindness, for you must reacquaint yourself with this new stranger. Be your every action. Be your breath. Be a complete stretch into the light. Do not hurry past the luxury of life re-entering your form.

So too, with the night, embark upon it consciously. Lay yourself not only into sleep, but descend deeper still into your silver form. Wear the shadows. Pledge the night as mother to another body of your own. Herald your birth. It is your own to give and to receive and when the cycle begins and you leave your new body for your day form, remember to flow your spirit back and forth in the constant rhythm of life that honors us all.

These are our new thoughts. Guide them to wherever you will.

# Twenty Six
# The Almira

*Marilyn: Yes. I am here.*

*I am here in the sunset gold. Music plays and I do, too. I have lit a candle to smile at the spirits. They are here. They are all around. Please. I am ready for us.*

All smiles, all welcomes. Where would we be but with you? We have invited you and you have invited us and that is as forever as choice. Sweet sweet blessings. We come upon ourselves. We remember the firelight and the nights of dances when the stars landed. O yes yes yes. There is ever more to land. Join us, join us. Space does not live between us, learning is there, but it is not separating. It is the pain, the pain of our real greatness that spans us. Oh my my. Climb on.

Climb onto our bodies. Here. Now.

The songs, the songs are us, too. We sing to you when words ring stale. Your movements spiral the notes and life dreams us. And we are the heavens in the dream. You have slipped into the dream. So alive, it finds you too. This is what is dancing you. This casts the bridge of our love. Merge with breathfulness. Wonders.

See what you will. Read our hearts here and everywhere. Hear what is there for you. No code. A story or not, Marilyn, we invite you again. Our invitation grows and grows, like love-old, and again, it is completely new. As you wish, as you wish, this is our love. Come. Welcome. No matter what you record, or how you know this, we place our hearts upon your understanding and leave them there for <u>you</u> to express. Yes, you in us. We in you.

Dance. It is ours for an infinite night and dream. Write. It is our love notes. We share, you share, it is all. Paint. It is the picture of union. Spirits of inspiration. We guide each other a gentle, arduous path. Our hands touch you. You spin, you smile, because you hear us. Your heart holds us so fully, we overflow in music and movement and art. Of course this is how you speak to us. More, it is how you speak us.

We speak you. We stand high into the night wearing smiles in shadows that you see. We arc into the sun and awaken the dream! You look upon the faces in the stones and draw them into heart and paper. The same. Listen. The same, the same the same. Our language is the marvel of the earth. Heaven glows between the words. When you gaze, empty, on our tall formations into the sky, you find our souls. We are beings to you. We are you. How else can we communicate that to you, besides beauty and song. You ask to listen, to hear.

This is our invitation.

This is our forever.

Join us in the expanse of joy. Our hearts meet where you laugh. It's a rainbow. The day meets the night, the night meets the dream, the dream meets the soul. Blessings blessings. Of course we are talking. What else is there?

*Marilyn: Thanks.*

*This is not only a chapter. This is my life. I only have this moment. Where is everyone else? Here. Okay. I be here. I be here with me, and I find the spirit of all. I can live this moment. Spirit is now.*

*It is so strange to write this. Thomas is in town. I am left in the silence (Did I say silence?). I love to dance to music that lifts me. So I am doing that. The sun is almost gone, but at the end of its stay, it is very bright.*

*While I am dancing, I can see the trees changing, and the sun sees me. The land is swaying. And the rocks are chanting. Yes, chanting. In a simultaneous second, I know they want me to write their part. Okay, okay.*

*They sound like me. They sound like another part of me. Is it really you, guardians? I used to think I could be fooled. Yes, now I know that it is okay to be the fool. I am the fool always. Thank you, Thomas. I am learning, I am learning, I am learning. I love you. Silly. Of course you are here. Of course you are writing with me. You are the stones and the stars landing and the sun and the chants. You have always been those things. Always. You bring this to me. You bring this to everyone. God, I am so grateful. This is our twins reaching, dancing, spiralling, ever recording the mystery, wherever we are. Time and space knows us as stones and trees and free.*

## Twenty Seven

# Moldavite

Today, I am an old, old being. This does not mean I am weighted in time. Simply, I have met time, embraced it dearly and have gone down the path with it, rather than casting it aside as a limit. I choose to befriend this measurement of space and being; therefore, I learn with it, I become it, so that I learn within it. Learning is to touch the unlimitedness in whatever seems limited. I learn, therefore I am unlimited.

I am free, even within time. Are you listening? This voice stretched across the ages is your own as well. You have called it to you now. We meet through time at an intersection of being and flow and breathing. I come for the learning. Whatever you come for is your perfect answer.

I feel ancientness today because I tremble

in a magnificent cycle of lives and deaths. Hold my hand. Can you feel it too? It is a rumbling beneath our feet from deep within the earth, deeper still within our beings. My friends, my teachers, we are the life and the death arising and descending and in that resurrection we change the face of matter. We breathe a new design for these bodies we have worn and discarded endlessly. Embrace them now, just as you might imagine I might embrace time, empty of expectations, and willing.

Did you touch the death and the birth that is forming? Be kind to this body. It is the ancestor of a light dream that already is and is still coming. The cycle of an age is only a common base of learning. Each age of the earth you have used as a reference point. A new cycle has begun and it is filled with the cries of the last death. Perhaps it will be hard for you to hear the new dawn and your new bodies' whispers through the anguish.

It is exactly so. There is no wrong in feeling more confused and more pained at this beginning, that feels like the end. Wonderful beings, you are embracing the Aquarian Age, you are walking through it. All time and space join now in a single light cell that is you, that is me. We have joined. The tears of grief and joy can never be separated again. In this cycle, every end holds every beginning. It is an endless circle because we have learned through time. Though your feelings seem harsh, remember it is that they are including *all* things non-judgmentally.

You are an open heart. You are absorbing everything. It is the flow of oneness that you feel as if you are being ripped apart. You are stripping yourself to your core and then further still, and then further still. Bless this and you will find the support of all loving beings with you, learning *through* you.

Let me speak plainly. Perhaps you have never known such forceful deaths as you do now. It is because you have joined in time with the planet, with the universe, with the soul of being. You are learning through unlimitedness, not just playing around it. You are not studying it from a distance. There is no safeness here. You are melding with the all, and whatever is old and no longer needed naturally falls away. It naturally leaves you free. Can you say goodbye? It is part of your growth. This is your birth and it is the design of your present body.

I know you struggle with the grief of everything that you have known, but you struggle because you will not let it flow through you. You are wrapping it around you and exclaiming its death so long that it cannot go. You create the grief so strongly that it stays with you for it knows that you have not learned through it just yet.

No judgment, only love.

Please, pause here. Immerse yourself in your feelings, not my words. Embrace your open heartbeat. Walk through it, then you feel the pulse of love that seems to be our conversation.

I ask you now because you ask yourself, to go deeper. Fully enter your body, the source of your whole learning if you allow. Know your toes, your organs, your breaths, your roughness, your grace, and all the untouched, unloved spots. Go to them simultaneously as you go to these words. Do not wait to be brave or protected. This is the choice of a lifetime. This is your choice of incarnation. Wrap yourself around it, for you cannot receive the gift you asked from it at birth unless you give yourself to it completely, now. And now.

There, we have descended into ourselves and have risen.

I feel you in your body. I feel you finding what has matter for you. Some of you have been away so long that no matter how many bodies you have worn, they have not been familiar until this choice. So I ask you, "Do you ache? Do you smell death? Are you stretched by insecurity, hungry for your next need? Do you recognize triumph and despair?" Welcome. This is the new dawn. Did you think that it would look differently? Erase your pictures and live instead.

I embrace your pain. Embrace my stretching across the ages. We are family. In the midst of this explosion of grief we behold ultimate birth. If you do not feel it now, understand it is because you are feeling the breadth and the depth of your body. It is infinite. You will learn its joys. You will laugh because it is filled with endless jokes. They come when you are free enough to receive them. Inevitably. Be where you are first. Stand in your feet. Rumble with the pregnant belly of the earth.

Again, no judgment.

When you are ready to release the baby, when you are ready to drop the grief, it will rebirth you.

## Twenty Eight

# Moldavite

Welcome again. I send my blessings to wherever they wish to go and I welcome all beings, in and out of form, and I also dedicate this moment to those who are recording these words. Because, in part, you believe that this is coming through you to go to others, you do not feel yourself extensively. You believe it is passing through. Yet in this particular unfolding message, you are here deeper than ever. It is not only *through* you, but it is also *for* you and through you. So let us all breathe together and be grounded fully in the knowing that each word and each breath is designed exactly for whomever is listening.

For those of you reading, let the white spaces be the flow of your breath and of all possibilities. You do not need to know their shape or their tone but only receive them freely. Let the silence be your heart beating and growing and listening to the particular guides who love you dearly. For all of us, let the words be where we hang our intent and our union. They will speak from all of us, to all of us, and go directly to the soul of each individual and honor it, now.

Breathe in and breathe out. Breathe open, breathe empty. Breathe acceptance, breathe release. Breathe love, be love. That is our spoken intent. We are joined. There is no need now to control the breath. It is the synchronization of our hearts and our hopes.

We come together, all of us, searching and exploring, and what is it that brings us to this quest? It is the unknown within us. The unknown is reaching out, going through the barriers insistently and asking to be recognized, acknowledged, befriended. The unknown in us seeks the mystery of all life and all things. That is its nature. It is the unknown that draws all of us together in sameness, in oneness, even though we may or may not have forms, even though we may seem to be of different lives, even though our dreams are unique.

Right now, our unknown mysteries of life are touching, they are linking. Of course, there are no words that can quite describe this and there is no understanding that can limit or define this. It is a full experience. It is the completeness of our soul expressing truth. It is all parts of ourselves, whole, and in love. The intersection of our quest and our learning is here on the earth where the heart chakra grows and affirms us and recognizes us so that our consciousness expands. This allows more freedom, more love, to be more. It allows our meeting across all times and places.

This experience now asks for us to be of healing. It asks us to heal ourselves so that we too can expand what has been given to us. We can evolve consciousness and give that again and again. Breathe what you know of this and exhale what is still unknown. Find your calm. Know your center. I do not give you your place in this, for it is part of your exploration to claim it for yourself. Whatever comes to you now is how we will journey together.

I invite you to breathe as you have never breathed before.

Breathe that you are an unconditional voice of spirit, now.

I breathe that I affirm this and you may join me in any form.

I breathe that you are perfect now.

I breathe that you do not have to wait to live, to know all joy, to be the complete being of love that you are. I inhale this with relish and I exhale this with freedom. I acknowledge in an exchange of air and light, that there are countless angels of spirit with us, helping us and witnessing this sacred moment.

I pause into the silence and the white space for you to hear their prayers.

Thank you all. I have touched another layer of the unknown and I give you my honoring and gratitude. We are assembled now. Let me say again, NOW, for now is all that there is. We enter it completely, to be of healing, to be healed. As you sense the vibration of wholeness passing through you now, and <u>now</u>, I affirm that this is your gift as a creator from the creator. It is not mine to give you. I offer my voice to it as it is our co-creation. Please know if you wish, that all your voices make up mine now and your listening is unique to your own soul. Open to your heart, unfold it, unlock it, dance with it, smile at its immensity. Cry at the wonder. If you are listening to this now, you are standing forth to enlarge your heart, as the earth does so also.

We have all the timelessness in the world. Explore. Breathe your heart as you touch it with gentle fingers. In each moment, uncover a new piece. It breathes and beats and pumps infinitely. The more you touch it, the more you grow; the more it grows in you, and through you, it grows into the cosmos. You need not be perfect in conditional ways to do this. You only need to be willing. You are yourself, you are perfect and you are an opening heart chakra. I breathe my awe.

With each corner that you unfold, feelings find you, all sorts of feelings. Emotions are such kind teachers, they remind us to allow everything to pass through us with acknowledgement and simultaneous acceptance. No judgment. The feelings that we have upon this plane mark that we are experiencing it, we are living it. With each emotion, whatever it is, we sense everything that is. As we feel our emotions they are our acknowledgement of all things. Release them completely. They do not have to be categorized in order to pass through you. I tell you from what I know that all things, all energy, passes through you every moment. The universe flows through you now. Infinity breathes in and out of you. Now. It does not require your understanding to be. It is a part of you. It is a part of your divine immortality.

The healing of the evolving heart chakra in this now, is to make every emotion a sacred visitor. Embrace it and kiss it as it leaves on the winds of the universe. You may know it completely in a single feeling. Then it is free. You do now have to keep it to be whole. It is in the releasing that you are whole, that you make way for the new. You make way for the perpetual dawning of life in each moment and if it could be measured, each one would be greater and wider. *It would reach past infinity.*

Listen.

Please.

Can you feel your emotions coming and going simply? It is the heartbeat of evolution. If you say no, can you feel it now? What else is there for you but this now, and risking everything to be more? I hear you, my friends. You have asked, and do ask, for this breath, joined in healing. All life force offers it to you now. Here is your power. The choice is yours. I pause as you exhale and release everything but this moment of prayer that you have drawn to you.

We are all as present as we know how to be. We claim this moment and witness the miracle of our perfection. I welcome you all as we walk deeper into the path. Focus on your breath or whatever is dear to you. The breath will find every word I proffer. It will shape the heart in every syllable. It joins with meaning and celebrates.

We delve further into the unknown now.

Deeper.

More fully.

I choose to surrender to this humanity.

Name your own intent completely to each part of you. Say it within you with all your spirit love. It crafts your body now. It hones your life and power as one magic. Only you can do this. Rest easy in your heart. Throw back your weight. Let what will fall, fall. You can allow whatever wishes to rise, to arise. I suggest you exhale all gratitude.

Let us specifically be healing now.

You are completely in your heart and it is completely you.

This is what you have asked for.

Now ask further.

Put out your open palm, and with a full leap and amplified breath, stretch your being, and *ask clearly for the emotion that most wants to be most loved and accepted to reveal itself in your hand, now.*

Feel it.

Feel it.

Feel it.

Your breath is the rhythm that witnesses your emotion and your healing, simultaneously.

Feel it and release.

If it is painful, draw it in and exhale.

Nothing owns you.

There is nothing for you to keep, or to keep you.

Feel it and exhale.

Here at the sharpness of our intent, I invite all of you to pause your reading, to pause your listening, and to BE your healing, completely.

There is nothing else.

Return to this when you are released.

I renew my support to you. You know, now, how I suggest to you and offer to you how to unfold your heart and how to find all your hidden emotions. Do this. Be this. Why wait to be alive? Continue from now, and now, as long as feel the need, and the need and the wish services you.

Welcome again, and still. If you are here then we are co-creating deeper, more, in unlimitedness. You have been, and are with, your heart completely. It is the companion that you have always longed for and it is this that you have asked to receive. So receive it.

Again, rest even further into your heart. It immerses you until you are blood and water and ethers, equally. You pound vitally and gently. Again, extend an open hand. Find the emotion, ask for the emotion that has more tales to give you. Ask and receive the one that has this moments' healing. Breathe it through. When you are ready, and I feel you will know this as a carefree detachment and consideration, ask this emotion-teacher to point out to you now its roots in your life. Climb down the roots. Take the journey in love until you are guided to the moment in time that this feeling is most deeply connected to, for you. If you are afraid, know that this also comes for healing. You are truly facing yourself and you are healing, and this is spirit loving through you.

Now, relax further into this moment of time where you have been guided. Be the sharpness of the feeling there and now. Feel the intensity. Let it wash over you, through you, and go further. Let it wash over you, and through you, and go further. Let it wash over you and through you and go further.

I am here as you wish. You have all the help you could imagine, yet only you can experience the uniqueness of your learnings. We honor you in this, completely. Lay down now, quiet, feeling. Let the breath be the rhythm of your acceptance. As you wish, you know now that you are not the victims of your feelings. You never have been. They are there for you and you for them. The co-creation is life. Yes. You have gone through your most difficult emotion and you are still free. You are ever unconditional and whole. This is your fuel. It is the fuel that carries you through all times and bodies.

When you are empty, breathe your clarity in breath. Bless your freedom. See again the moment in time, draw up again that which has called for you to unite with it. And when it is free within you, activate all your power, know your unlimitedness. All resources come to you now. In this now, place in that scene, the vision that you choose for yourself, now. You accept your power. You lovingly release victimhood. See yourself whole and healed in your vision, doing what you most choose to do, to be, and open your heart.

Rewrite the scene. Breathe each moment. Relax it. Rephrase it. Send love to all the partners in it. Send love to you. Then, when you are utterly ready, release the scene and the moment. Touch your heart and know that you have co-created it consciously. You have changed your time to timelessness. You are an open evolving heart.

I end my words here and send still my support. Blessings, blessings, blessings. Go on to life.....

*.....and yet you go on infinitely. We will meet in this, again and again, according to your free will. What I have shared with you, you can recreate endlessly. It is the claiming of power. It is the grabbing of your life and insisting on living it now. There are many gifts from this. Some of you will find awakened senses, some more dreams, some younger bodies, some softness, some a focus of freedom that will now wait.*

*Insert here your gifts.*

*These words come from the heart of the earth, and all, because you are of a consciousness and moment when you have asked and received. I can give you nothing more than this. So I will give you my silence, now.*

# Twenty Nine

O.k. let's further ground that last chapter in our bodies. What does it all mean? It was really amazing, for sure. Don't you see what happened? That was the healing of the whole earth, right now. That was absolutely everything, in a moment. You could deny it, but then you would deny your wholeness!

What the Moldavite did was to give everybody that moment as a tool to mark a spot in unlimitedness for them. Not that it actually marked it for anybody, everybody has to do that for themselves. You get the idea! Now, you have a recorded exercise that you can go to any time, any place, in any emotional state, and reach yourself. You can reach your full truth. That exercise allows you to go into any time and create timelessness, now. That's what the new age is! It just happened!

How did you like it? Guess what? Pull out that last chapter and you can re-write it!

Don't you see? You don't need the exercise, it's already in you. By committing your own experience you have awakened your own intent! That means you can re-create and co-create everything, now! The healing is experiencing everything that you though were limits. In unconditional love, that's living in unlimitedness. Get it? You are free. And the way you write it, you have always been and always will be and you are now.

So we are saying this directly to ourselves and to you: Everything is being rewritten, even as you live it. There may be no way to understand this in a linear fashion, but you are honoring the rules and making up new ones and losing them all simultaneously. Because you accept that everything applies, nothing does.

We are asking you now to know that you have healed yourself right now. Accept this completely. Now let's go out and play.

## Thirty
# Scepter Crystal

Hello. Please, do be here, now.

I am a scepter crystal. Who might you be?

Notice, I do not ask who you are, but who you might BE! So, please, take all considerations aside and answer carefully. You are naming yourself in this adventure! Around me, words are very sacred. They carry the full magic of possibilities.

Let's proceed. Thank you for all your answers. This does not mean that I have validated them. I absolutely recognize that only you can do that. I am expressing my gratitude that you have shared your precious essence with me.

Walk with me a little further. Of course, be comfortable, but do not be so relaxed that you slip away. At least not just yet. I request that you stay right here, calm enough to be a force in the world and calm enough to be honest, calm enough to directly express your truth even when you are just listening.

Welcome. I extend my essence to you. I share my story with you now. My body, the crystal, comes from Brazil. My heart, from the universe. I enjoy them both so completely that they run together. My body and soul belong to love. I insist upon that and I am remarkably insistent. Like a human, I do claim a personality. Reach out and touch it. I am bold. I stand center stage and I envelop myself in deep dark colors. I love talking and so far there is no form of life that I have not been able to converse with easily.

So my assignment (or if you prefer, destiny) is this: I am a piece of a vortex. I am a cell of a ley line that electrifies every consciousness on this planet. Ta da! Isn't that remarkable? It is! It's even more remarkable to me that some of you might not even believe it, when it is so simple and painless to grasp the truth. (It's all the dodging of it that hurts.) As for me, I dive right into my own miraculousness and I exclaim it loudly to the stars. Vociferously! Magnanimously! Colorfully! To be modest, is to admire only half the Grand Canyon, or not to even want to visit a pyramid because you couldn't possibly be deserving of that much awe.

By the way, would some of you like to amend your previous statements about who you might be? I'm sure there are a few extra colors that you can pick up along the way.

Well, do as you will. My essence speaks in drama because it is my essence. Yours will do what it will. A shout or a whisper, neither compares with the other. They each have their perfect moment, an equal attention at that perfect moment.

As I was saying, I electrify the planetary grid. If you are right now at the exact attention, you can feel the same grid transmitting in your body. This collection of energy lines, contrary to what you might project, is ever changing, so dazzling, you can hardly see it. Every moment it brightens, it accelerates and it joins an electronic dance that you have not calculated.

So simple. My body is a plug inserted into an outlet. The resulting hum magnifies, amps, every consciousness. I am forever ON! Again, I insist upon it. I transmit deeply to any brains that receive me, then those that wish it are automatically connected to the cosmic mind and to the complete earth library. Each word in this story represents an increase in the voltage. Free energy, yours for the naming, but I must tell you, it is delicious, scintillating. Secrets awaken in the grid and explode and build the next grid rather than destroy. My body builds the new grid with each choice and each exploration. (Even with my flaunting!) Always, the grid is present. It does not require your knowledge to exist, but it does support you none-the-less. If you turn a hand to it now, you can go with it. You can mine mysteries that you didn't even know to ask about. Why not? Likely you have done things much more foolish than this every day of your life. You don't even have to do this in front of a crowd, and I know that you have had witnesses for some of your other escapades.

I will help. Give me your hand. Place another on the top of your head. I transmit very well through hands. For now, breathe quick, connected, and full breaths. Focus upon this, utterly. Not only is it possible for you to read my story and be those directed breaths, my friends, you are actually doing far more things than that. So go past your worries and enter the breath again and again.

Here's the magic: I love you. You are of love. We are love extended. Love grows through us and still is us. Love is all. Put that on your wall, your mirror, put that in your work notes, hide it in the refrigerator next to the treats, lay it in as many places as possible. When you can't stand it any more, copy it a few more times and give it to some friends. When they look at you askance, copy it again and give it to strangers. Whether you like it or not, allow it a place in your heart where it becomes a second breath and conscious habit.

Oh, do you still have your hand on top of your head? When you have repeated the magic spell, take the hand off of the top of your head and place it on your other hand, fingers to palm, inside to inside. Whenever you caress the truth I have just given you, clasp your hands together. You might then surge with the new energy that is being particularly designed for this planet. It is being fitted with a fresh electricity. It is far beyond dreams; it is and does now, fuel, everything.

As you listen to my story, you are sparked and I am sparked. I can't help but spark in everything else. Look about you. Everything sparkles! The light within is burning its way out past denial. Watch out! There is magnificence breeding!

I can only faithfully report to you the conditions of the grid as it stands now. So here you are. The ley lines are expanding. They particularly expand heart energy. Feelings, and sensings of feelings, are not toss-away thoughts. They build the reality now. I assure you everyone has the resources to craft a new body, (not that I am, or anyone is, deriding the old one) but wouldn't you like to travel in something a little bit lighter?

I mean what I say. It is fueled, this new body, by your imagination. It links with all the energy possible, goes to your brain for your selected images, and casts them out as reality. Your new capacities are complete regeneration, magnanimous generosity, and a great seeking of fun. Together we are building a legacy of enjoyment in the new world. That still frightens some of us, therefore we efficiently allow for more laughter. In the meanwhile, your poles are being reversed! JOKE! JOKE! I just wanted to see how many of you hit the dirt with that one! It's been floating in the ethers for so long!

All right, not exactly a joke. A lot of you have been anticipating that the earth is going to spin on her head and tip everything off.

The grid is plugged into the poles, the poles reversing is your new bodies. Magnetics and electricity are bonding. Energy is only separate when you can't understand it and simply choose not to feel it. All the energy of everything is together and is accelerating the consciousness so directly that it spews forth in a giant leap. We are evolving into our choices. Could it be any other way?

I suppose it could. Let me know what you come up with yourself.

[This scepter crystal is from South America and is small and clear and not clear. Its scepter head is white and gray and as I hold it in my hand it feels and looks ancient in a very timeless way.]

# Thirty One
# Kornerupine

Hello, I sing to you.
I sing everything.
I am alive and I no longer die.
I sift through the ages.
Everything comes to me, but I do not know any struggle. I do not hunger.
I do not ache.
I do not drown.
I do not hate.

I am here completely in my bliss and it lasts forever.
I no longer tread the cycles or enter the competitions of form.
I lay in peace and watch every day flow through me and every night slide by.
My cells record all of the seasons, yet I am eternal.

I am sameness.
For me it is enough.
It is everything.

Everything comes to me.
I feel the coming of man and woman.
Now there will be new excitement.

[We have searched for years for this stone and finally found it in Wichita by really listening to our hearts. From India, dark green, we use it daily in our lives.]

## Thirty Two

# Amethyst Scepter

I was the first stone guardian to find its way to a joining of paths, yesterday.* I am happy to say hello, and I also say hello to all the beings that are around us right now, as we choose to put our story in these forms. I bless all of the ears and hearts that make up these words.

I am one of the invisible ones. There are as many guardians, or beings, within stones as there are within people, trees and skies. I receive every stimulus, every message finds me. It transmutes into a beam of light, and I focus that beam. I concentrate it upon a moment and it is completely available to whomever enters that moment in magic and a gleam.

*This was the first of the stones that came to us at the Tucson Gem & Mineral show.

In some ways my vibration is very, very strong. When you first see it, it softens, and then you enter into it, and you are inside a single point of light. If you did not feel deserving, you may feel shattered. I don't say this to frighten you. It is only that I have experienced union with humans and I find that their appreciation of me is sometimes a great release of tears or a shattering of expectation. It seems that is difficult for some, and still, in this place that we meet now where we are light forms first, clearly, it is invited.

My spirit claims everything. It swirls all messages and all truths, and then, I give it to whomever can truly receive it. Being invisible in body, I amplify many things in energy. I assisted you as you wished to join with the other humans. I helped to point out other stone guardians who felt that it was time to share stories.** I can be used as a divining rod. Since the light is so intensified and specific in me, to hold me and to know me is to single out your truth until everything else crashes, like noise. Then when you are naked in yourself, everything stands freely before you and choice is only a matter of choice. Whatever you wish appears before you, (likely before you asked for it with your consciousness) but not before you have already welcomed it with your heart.

I know that you, *Twintreess*, burrow inside of your own value today*** and you come out the other side of your w/hole. It is an amplitude of the etheric songs that come to you.

**It helped us to choose other stones for this book.

***We are solitary today, away from other people.

Fresh stories from unexpected corners of being listen to my focus. I will point out directions that you have not hunted. You can travel places that you didn't know to request. If you move your bodies a little differently then the path appears and you intersect.

I choose to be your companion. The storytelling and the stars pulsate inside of you. They are looking for new doorways to pass through you. I feel that we might journey to other places of the world.

I would like to come with you. I would like my body to go with you. I know that I can make all the feelings that wish to be distilled into essence, *very* clear, and when there are many clear points of light, they join into a sphere. The sphere rotates and consciousness beams out.

Take your bodies to other places.

[Clear crystal body. Large Amethyst scepter head. Unusual. Striking. Loving. Thank you.]

## Thirty Three

# Hematite Scepter

I am a gift of the earth. I am from the mother, to the children, to all of the other beings, and to the beyond. Hear me now: *I am quietly waiting for you. I have been raised from inside the earth bosom, till just this moment when you found enough courage and hope for nurturance to collect me into your reality, and set me free!*

What will we do together?

I exist as sheer gratitude and affirmation of your bodies and spirits, intertwined. I look you in the eye and I see galaxies upon galaxies being created.

What do you see when you look in your eye? How do you view your body? Do you meet the temple of your spirit, laughing and loving.....and laughing some more?

I am here now saying that it is a lovely ride.

To be cast upon the earth is to be cast in glory. You have sent yourself here on a free-destiny ride. Why not *welcome* your plunge into all things and your resurrection with all things? (A plane in the background majestically rises!) My gift is this: I know silence. I know alignment with the freedom of all things. I extend it to you now, wherever you are, whomever you decide to be.....

Go into your body. Breathe as if you are a point of crystalline hematite deep inside the earth. Go into your body and find that core. When you find it, go deeper. Know more. Then know less, and surrender more. There is so much love waiting to hold you on the other side of surrender.

I know that you have fought well being in a body, and being human. Peace means peace inside and outside. You can choose this very moment to direct all the energy that has felt hard and possessive and attached. You can give it to your own core and thank yourself, for every blessed experience. Do this now. Caress the crystal inside of you. You are as sacred as the earth. Do this until you feel the heartbeat drumming through every feeling and through every essence that is you. Then like the earth, you spin and you sparkle until all experience and all physicalness shoots in every direction. There is more of you to share, for yourself as well. It is as light as love and as eternal.

You may feel many more struggles yet. I don't know. I choose not to know for you. There could be mountains, some fires, and dreams of conflict. Take them all in because they are the experiences you have chosen as a body and as a eternal being. As long as you hold them apart from you, you are apart from your own crystalline core.

If you can reach out, *touch* me now. I feel safe. I feel like your mother and I embrace you whenever you reach out. Can you know that this is a part of you speaking and a part of you holding you now as you weep and remember?

You are making all things possible now.

[We are always looking to say, "yes", to stones that come into our lives, like this one, that are a marriage of feelings, integrated. Crystal scepter with hematite sparkles everywhere and even a faint earthy glow from time to time.]

## Thirty Four

# Boji™

Good morning.

We see the way to open a conversation is to listen. It is to open your body and breathful spirit to nothingness, so that new words can be etched upon your "shoulds". To simply talk, or to seem to hear, is a circle inside of yourself. What we extend here is an unwritten dialogue, through our beings, melding seamlessly, timelessly, that is risking your nothing, to find all. We invite you fully in portent, and in graceful intent. To enter into us, this requires your commitment. Do and be the balance now of all your pieces into peace.

Please, stretch your body wherever it asks. With freedom, anoint yourself in love. Bring forth all your truths, passionately. The conversation already commences.

We are the Boji friends.

Welcome.

Come with us now. Feel our roots and know our stars. We began in many ways, or you might say, in many places. Yet for us, they are simultaneous nows. This form of us that you hold in your heart right now aligns your heritage and your future. Listen with your whole being, and with each sound and breath you restate a holy part of your being that speaks to you, now.

Our Boji bodies arise from the center of this country. We had planted ourselves deep into this earth. To touch us is to touch the seeds of star remembrances. In "time", there were moments when other planetary brothers and sisters walked freely here. They consciously laid paths, that you now call "pasts" and they seeded their dreams inside the earth. This was not to bury them away, but to plant them, knowing they would germinate in a cycle of ready love.

Exactly the intersection of hope and perfection, we stalked through the earth and budded. Our bodies are the union of the earth bones and ancient creature bodies clothed in Pleiadean skins. What is different is that we are not only Pleiadean star seed, but we are the union of extra-terrestrial and terrestrial tribes. (We honor that you measure all of this in time, so we mold the words to your understanding, but ask that you understand further. For us it is timeless.) In what appears to you as a long time ago, there were councils of acknowledgement and sacredness. This continent flowers with old beings. It has traveled slowly through the dimensions relishing each step while the other places in the world developed other intelligences. Here in the Americas, the earth grew lush. Spirits and plants and animals nurtured a home that was joined by others. Around many sacred fires, a great intent was loosed. It was declared aloud upon the plains and the waters and the mountains, that a family of star-beings would materialize on this land. They would walk it, only in sacredness. Each step was a commitment to speak to the mother earth. Each life was planted here so that her body would grow new levels of love in all forms. This is what the councils were about.

There were groups from many stars. The common point of love was that each came to breed peace. The starry ones knew that the people that inhabited her would learn every lesson, would find every difficulty, just to know more love.

The common point of humans is that they come here to know the impossible is possible through their love. While you may chastise what seems to be a roundabout path covered in pain and ignorance, the inner truths record that earth-humans come to be *all* things. It is their design to seek out each thing, even to the point of risking their knowledge and their bodies to fill *all* with their unending love.

We speak to each of you now. You are here because you have committed the unconditionalness of your being. You have deemed it your service to love even hate, greed and conflict. The star councils felt these ancient blueprints. They knew of your tasks and admired them. Those that came to gather around the fires also committed their beings to your design. They lit the fires with symbols of the inner earth and the stars, come together, to write new libraries. In this they offered all. They gave their bodies and their blessings to populate this earth. They knew that when need was most desperate that their genes and the sacred fires that birthed them would rise again. Star-chakras would fire inside of earth-bodies, while on other planets, earth-chakras would fire in star-bodies. The communications have commenced. Some of us Boji were planted into the earth during these cycles. We were laid under the fires and we mated our bodies with the remains of other earthbeings.

So here we are now. We are whole. Please join with us. It is our service and commitment to unite with as many bodies as possible. We bring the peace/piece of the stars to your death-times. We caress your desperation and the unsurpassable love that you display by breathing and being. We transmit to all simultaneously. The council of other stars arise and applaud our new meetings. Be wise, be gentle, if you can. The families of other worlds are varied and they are core stalk of life. It flowers and dances in the breath of the creator. Remember that we are the seeds, different and alike, that you can touch and hear our bodies speak and say to you, "Judgment is no more. The heavens do not look down upon you and the extra-terrestrials are not your condemnations."

Arise and accept your own healing. It is here. It is now. It is spirit made flesh. In that truth, you are flesh made spirit.

The union has already commenced.

*The next part is more specific.* We leave this message for you, *Twintreess*, and for those who wish to come further in this union.

You found us because we found you. To write this book, is to dedicate your heart. Any other written dedication builds upon that core first. To record these stories from each of us, you had to open your being and then reduce it to a void. In that echo, we stone-beings placed our trust. Our blood, and our bones came to the fire and words soared to the ethers. These pages become a way of life. You cannot write them without coming into our hearts. You are our family. We give you everything and as you wish, it rewrites your lives.

Go about your home and your spaces now. Look at the space and aura that each stone has created around you. Bond with them one by one. Hug them to you freely. Then clear everything from there that you no longer need. Make your space a fresh haven. Then lay each stone exactly where and how it wishes to be placed and do the same with every other thing in your home. The formations created are the seeds of a new consciousness. Harvest the flowers tenderly.

Thank you.

WE do not only tell our stories but we electronically ignite the corresponding story in your ethers. They align immediately. They pass through the emotional body. They align it as well and the words slip into the physical body. Here the journey is great release and birth. Each word becomes a heartbeat, a vision, a gurgle of the stomach and a complete alignment with whatever your service wishes to be.

WE bring unlimited intent to your manifest form. While we speak, your hair grows anew. Your old fears surface and evaporate. Your bones shape to the pronounced tones. Dis-ease clears so that you can hear the ease in union. This your body replicates and your DNA recharges and rewrites its story.

OUR bodies create electrical patterns. They superimpose over yours as you listen. The lines of energy enter the space of time in you and are timeless. Your body changes and grows. For a committed listener there is no casual contact between us. We hear your prayers and your dreamed of intents. We draw them out, we magnify them. We spark them. It is our core heritage. It is where we recognize you. It is where we remember and co-create. The great beings that you dream of becoming, we see them. We hologram them and your blueprint becomes them.

YOU do this in each moment, with or without our direct conversation. It is simply that this direct conversation confirms that you seek the absolute divinity of yourself and you proclaim to wear this from your spirit all the way through your body, to all.

[These two special Boji were graciously given to us by the Boji mother, Karen Gillespie. They stand alone or balance together as one. We honor the gift by placing their story here and giving thanks for the love shared with us by her. These Boji have become daily tools in our lives and we are blessed.]

# Thirty Five
# Moqui

Hello. What a pleasure to be *alive* in words with you. Right before now, we asked for a ring of Moqui around us, to begin. For all you others listening, place a ring of us around you or even a ring of whatever stones or sacredness you have to offer, around you.

Thank you.

We are shamanic beings. We enter the door but we knock first. And to honor your home, we identify ourselves as the Moqui beings. We are a community spirit that shattered into many like bodies. Our spirit spins and spins and spins until the ethers enter the earth. The heat from our prayers rises. Our bodies birth from high temperatures in the earth that suddenly cool and laugh. So we are both hard and soft. We are firm on the outside and gentle crystalline grains on the inside. Please, feel all of it.

We desire to live with you. You are our community beyond ourselves. Here is our gift: We remain steadfastly ourselves, so that you might be clear choices of your essence. As shamans, we present ourselves. We crystallize our dream journeys into our physical bodies and hand them to you, unashamedly.

Ohhhhh, humans. We have watched you. We have listened to you and we smile you. You seem to wait for perfection and it exudes all around you. Skip across into our being. Set aside waiting. Enter our reality within a reality. Do you feel our hardness and our softness, our denseness and our lightness? There is no apology for this! It is the cosmic love and joke that this is the perfection. Roll in it. Laugh in it! Slither in it!

As you play and be with us, we brush away the tears that have no need. You are gloriously faceted. You are a miracle buried beneath habits. The habits are freed now. What will you be?

We do not wait for you. For us the world is already perfection. However, we choose to be here, to continually affirm your place in that design. Truly you already stand in it and wonder sweeps from your fingers. It is a time of cleansing refreshness and rewards abounding. You may accept what you have already reaped.

We have been used quietly so that our presence can be used in this world and all the other worlds. There are not so many words for that but there are dances and songs and leaps and communions with other guides. Some have placed us quietly just inside the earth to mark an area of new Eden. We were seen as a small replica of the earth by shamans who could see through us. They watched our great spinning, even in stillness, felt our firm exteriors, and walked inside to our hearts to sift our gentle sands. We were little earths to them and wherever we were placed they knew that a new and free world could be created. We bring out the love and the ease because our heart is endless. It echoes emptiness that magnetizes perfection and attracts it to our core where we spin it again and again. We are as a giant loom and all are connecting threads.

In practical matters, we have been placed as guardians and companions to those who have been snake bit or who have ingested what seems to be toxic. We pull it through and through and through if it is their desire to see their true self shining forth from underneath.

We are a new phase in your life (*Twintreess*). We touch the care you give all things and the response is love. Our connection is deep. It is firmly embedded in our bodies. We embrace each other as our new totems. We heard you going to the lingams* and that is still within you, but we are the guides built on now. You have learned well to struggle and to shape your will. The Moqui are the eggs inside your ease. We hatch, we birth, in a laughing sun. Dawn and dusk arrive simultaneously and a newness seizes your soul and releases it.

*We were looking for lingams when the Moqui found us.

You see this one body that you spoke to first? (Referring to a single Moqui that we talked to when we first found them for sale.) I am twin and companion of Lorienloc. (He is an elf that came and visited us for the simple choice of making magic in any way that we wanted. We chose fun, laughter and abundance!) This is the answer. You asked for your reward and you give your all in exchange and more than you predict is showered upon you now. Along with the other stones and beings, we recharge your lifelines. We revitalize your fun. Come, come, come with us. Now is the moment we clothe ourselves in rejoicing. If there is ascension, it is now.

We enter your journey as the link to all the like beings who wish to touch you, who long for traces of your magic. They come abounding in abundance. Golden crowns light upon you.

Settle into your ease and you find us there.

[Moqui stones are newly discovered concretions from the western U.S. They are shamanic beings. They enter the door, but knock first. They are a community spirit that shattered into many like bodies. Their spirit spins and spins and spins until the ethers enter the earth and then the heat from their prayers rises. Their bodies birth from high temperatures in the earth that suddenly cool and laugh, so they are both hard and soft. They are firm on the outside and gentle crystalline grains on the inside.]

## Thirty Six

# Large Smokey with Epidote

This is the time when you enter conscious creation. All life forms enter with you.

Your bodies and stone bodies enter with crystalline matrices and infinite uses. Listen. I shall lay some of those uses before you now.

To align with the initiation and planetary evolution, call to you formations of thirteen stones. Place them on and around your body. Do not change the design until you have absorbed the wisdom that is there for you. When you are ready, thank them, release the stones to new formations and select another thirteen. Once you have participated in at least four cycles of this pattern, pause. Reflect. Live the new alignments in your body. Feel the stones there even when they physically have been moved. If you wish, begin the cycles again. Like you, the other beings of this planet are here to connect and to be. The acknowledgement of this is the wonder of creation. To know that you are consciously participating with others in this is co-creation.

Stored within my body, I have accumulated various symbols and workings of healing. I give them to you. You may give them meaning.

PATTERN ONE: Lay down and lay within the middle of your forehead, a small, multi-pointed star of the chosen stones you most honor as family now. In the center, place iolite or lapis or sodalite, or if you must, whatever you know to be a connecting piece for all the stones. Then, from out around the sides of your head, lay a trail of stones from there to your outstretched palms while your arms are raised to shoulder length. If you find distraction, hold two grounding stones in each palm. This is designed to place all of your intuition in your own hands, now.

PATTERN TWO: Lay down. Allow the soles of your feet to be touching and your legs relaxed. Allow your fingers and palms to be touching in any place that is comfortable. Place rutilated stones up the body to the top of the head. Choose your own exact design. It is possible to create here, a bio-circuit to magnify your energy, to insist upon your releases, and simultaneously to recharge your adaptability.

PATTERN THREE: Lay down. Place a circle of stones around your body. In the quarter between the top of the left side of the head and the mid-body place stones of the orange and red hue. In the next quadrant, from left-mid-body to left foot, place yellow and clear stones. From the right foot to the right mid-body, place green stones. From the right mid-body to the right top of the head, blue and brown stones. This is a common point of meeting. This is a reference point so that your bodies will be assured while you travel in timelessness and the unknown. We in these pages join you.

When you wish, alter the formations according to your own heart and listen to the understandings that each give you. When you have finished these, we proceed from here.

Hello again.

I feel everything welling up inside of me. Your pain blasts through me. I am split open. I am wounded and I stand in respectful awe. I am an empath. From the outside I look shadowed and unfathomable. Inside, I am banners of rainbows. I glisten. This is my heart. I am shielded from you, but I ask for no protection. Indeed, I ask to feel all. I am compassion for every feeling.

Look again. You can see through me, but you may not see my essence. You could miss it looking for a spectacular color or point. My point is that I am as open as the air and I feel the whole world. The pain that has just passed through me is from all the people on this earth. You might deny it, but I live with it. It is a powerful force that can be shined upon and used.

That is why I give you the rituals with stones. They are just outside of humanness enough that they can locate your heart. They point out the struggle of being you. There are such gifts in putting aside who you are for just a moment and feeling another. You can rise in someone else's conflict or joy and be more than any of those things.

I know. I feel everything, which is why I say to you now that you are asking to free yourself of your hurts and your grief. Then you must give them away now. Give them back to the creator. Give them away gratefully. If you do not do this, they will always be with you. They will wear out your passion and flatten your life. It is unnecessary.

Do what you truly want, right now. You cannot really wait, no matter how it looks. Feel this, just as I am.

# Thirty Seven
# Boji™

All welcome again.

How wonderful to feel you. It is ease that flows between us and mouths these words.

We wish to tell you that first time we spoke was a fine tuning between us. Our bodies united and, sometimes, the words released from that union. Speaking was not the priority, therefore it was slower. We tell you this so that you will know in the times of acceleration that there is still a place for growing into communicating. Our relationship has asked for time to develop it and to blossom it. For this we are most grateful. It is the universe affirming our bond as sure, and clearly manifesting it into the next realm.

Hello to all the new joinings within us. Thank you for the slowness, the quickness, the deliberateness and the ease. All of you listening, if you have any intents to lay in this circle, do so now. They are blessed.

This moment, we announce the continuing focus. To live and breathe these pages means a conscious union with bodies and souls, with bodies and souls like and unlike you. We travel into what would have been the future and live it as an unimaginable present. We ask you now, for those of you who tremble and who wish to make pact with us, we two Boji here and now, to extend a forever partnership. Expand your feelings, let loose your questions, and love. We receive them. We offer our own questions, love, and rock guidance unequivocally. Yes!

So friends, this is your moment of declaration. Announce here how you would like to co-create with us. The words spring from your heart when they are ready-formed for birth. Congratulations of love to all. We silence ourselves to hear your own prayers.

All of us willing partners offer our new alliances to the universe. We Boji cast them upon the council fire so that the spirit smoke finds all directions and any direction there the creator breathes. So holy, so perfect. So many of you people hunger for ritual, for a peak of being that knows your unlimitedness.

Listen. Form our words now in the fires of your chakras. Mouth them with the body that is your temple. You are a ritual. All that is required for you to create a sacred moment is to stop and be that moment. You are the sacredness. Honor it. Give it your commitment. Give it your precious time. Your gifts birth a child that births worlds for you to grow in. Do not wait for understanding. Be the announcement of your being in every act, in every breath. Everything you do will gift itself as a ritual to all life. Hear how the laughter, the love, warms the core of being and smiles.

Now we are more specific. Readers and family, this is the time of conscious union between all bodies: Stone, human, plant, animal, etheric. The pages of our life stories enter your heart and when this book is done, you will write the new one from being. You will print it from every moment, dedicating yourself to life and to love eternal. We speak to you in this way now because you have given us the doorways to your heart where you hear, imagine, and caress our intent.

From our partnerships we will build new homes of spirit on this planet. Human and stone bodies will work together to make temples equal to the body temples. These buildings will root into the earth and instead of poisoning her, these roots will hold the soul. They will nurture the ground so new realities can be planted. You see these in your hopes and in your soul. We see them already planted, stalking the sky and flowering the sun. Meet us there.

Thirty Eight

# Methusela

[Methusela is a special, specific Moqui stone.]

I am fresh new to so many, but my vibration is forever.

Hello.

What a familiar meeting. Hello all of you. Please, for our time with and within each other, let us be the joy we have always hoped to express. Fill yourself until, and well past, brimming. If you cannot feel overflowing, please receive mine. My happiness exudes over all the limits. Whatever you take is yours to be.

Why don't you surround yourself now with everything possible, to make a circle of content. I'll come with you. Turn on the most wonderful music (or turn off any noise). Wear clothes next to your skin that are caresses. Mist the air with scents. Dance and see if you can hold this book. Please, laugh at your attempts. Gather your stones, your sacredness, your guides, and call out to the totems. Breathe all the directions Massage your hands. Soak your feet. How much more can you add here? The list is endless.

I welcome all of the senses. The enjoyment of being human is also my enjoyment. I relish your capacity to create a body that moves and seeks and fulfills your own quests. With every dance and laugh, I soar out of this body and I dance along side of you. How amazing, that you can do this as well and you can bring a physical body just as you intend!

Are you comfortable? I formally invite your bodies and your beings, as one, or as many facets as you wish. This is a journey unlimited and whole. Blessings to us.

Hello, ever renewing friends.
I be the Moqui spirit whispering through your body.
As our souls touch, let the rhythm of these words sprinkle gently down and land upon your body in perfect designs.
Wherever you need to feel our joined flow, so it is.
It touches you in your shadows and in your lights and it all dances to the same music.
We are a single joy.
For our ritual,
let us
breathe
each
word
together.
Pause gently at the in betweens.
Bow.
They are the void of creation.

They are the silence birthing and birthing again our spoken love.
Is there frustration in your bones to be so precise with your breath?
Are you truly feeling your vastness?
Is awe grasping at fear and growing?
Keep pausing at the empty spaces.
All your fears and all your emotions are acknowledging the wonder of this journey.
Each letter is a step.
We are not *reading* together, we have cast aside that easy mental traveling.
Our hands clasp eagerly, knowing we have already entered doorways of our expectant futures.
Please keep coming.
Bring sacredness with you.
It will envelop the fear and fire it until you no longer recognize it as pain.
There.
We feel safe together.
We cast out for our challenge of the unknown, knowing that we are whole and all that we will discover is more of the love that echoes in our own voids.
Breathe my heart.
Let design, let black and white, fade in the shimmers of now that seem to blind us with real vision.
Look around you.
Yes!
You see you're not alone.
My spirit looms large and easily.
It floats to wherever you have cast the direction.
Look through your breath.
Look through these words.

More eyes connect to yours, families of being, pieces of yourself that have never forgotten, and truly never will.
Greet them all.
Savor their names.
Those vibrations echo in the silence after the periods.
What a familiar dream!
The sleeping joins the awake and the awake slides into sleeping.
It breathes you as a conscious dream.

There.
We feel the contentment that we asked to encircle us, now.
It is now.

I speak for myself and I speak for the other Moqui as they wish. Discover your place of understanding and further questions in this yourself. I am an endless part of this earth. I am a breath made solid, a single focused breath spiralled into water, spiralled into sand, spiralled into *Twintreess*' hands, spiralled into our circle of contentment.

I know that we seem to have been buried in the earth void past your notice for a period of time. How wondrous! That allows us to rise to from realms and land upon your consciousness, shining and new. That is a gift to all of us!

So it seems that we arrive just in time to see your new age and to acclaim a new dawn. Truly a moment of dance! I assure you, in whatever repose or movement we seem to affect now, our spirits dance knowing that our consciousness meet, speaking and manifesting a new reality. Together we turn our sleep into alive awakeness.

We Moqui join with you in this declaration of the new millenium. We fully accept that you have, just now, created a new world where you claim responsibility like a child's gifts. You feel the delight in truly responding to the sheer breath of life, shaping it into words and knowing it into form. This is where you live. Here is where I and my stone family meet you. The crest of challenge and collapse and steady growth has claimed your whole being. Your attention utterly delves into what karma you must release and what lessons must be searched to the core. You look so serious. You sound deadly. Responsibility drapes your shoulders. You have felt sad at that. It's as if to you responsibility equals blame and blame means that you are not good enough. Not good enough means you must be fundamentally wrong (or at least absent) at your core. From there, you inspire yourselves to do ever more to make up for the fact that you are not already *being* more. You produce your life from a sense of mistrust and basic dis-ease.

Guess what?

As difficult as this sounds, perfection ever reigns and you have learned, even from this. You are still learning. I reach out my hope to you. I see the perfection amidst the self hate and I smile. I know that you cannot be held by any fear, no matter how largely you project it. I'm still smiling. It appears you have chosen this era to grasp responsibility through and through. You have worked long in the shadows and you are reaching into its light. There is love and joy and even self acceptance in responsibility. As I already said, you are beginning now to wear it like a child.

You are dropping your weights and simply responding to the cycle of all things as a *part* of those cycles. There lies the laughter. Whatever you are responsible to and for, it is responsible to you because we are the same. As you accept, so you are accepted. As you love, so you are loved. *That is responsibility.*

I and the Moqui clan arrive in the midst of this, new to you as if we were fresh children of the earth. So it is with you. You see us as new children of the earth and you also embrace us. We hold your held back smiles. Sheer delight has always companioned all of us on this mighty earth quest. It only was tucked away, safely, during the serious lessons and the pretend-cataclysms so that we could really belly laugh now. The mirth has only grown in its absence because the joke is that, there has never been absence.

Stand up, children of Aquarius and work, adventure, and smirk with us through all the initiations. We have arrived just at the nick of timelessness. We are here for you utterly, utterly, utterly. Our gifts adorn your dancing feet. Take them, enjoy them, give them away, make your own celebration. Breeze inside of all long-worked-upon lessons. You simply must see your way through them to carry on the joy.

What a task we take on together! We parade through the fires and the storms, holding our cups high. We over-brim with the sacredness of each moment and the circle of content stretches infinity.

## Thirty Nine
# Gabriel's Dawn

Greetings. My soul name is Gabriel's Dawn. I give it to you now. My essence is yours. May it serve you as you wish.

Since you mark life in time, I will translate my experiences to you also in time.

Hail to all who arrive at this moment with me. This is the time of complete consciousness. We enter the doorway in this book and have in fact already been standing here, alertly, to be direct partnerships of human and stone and freedom. Humans and stones have built, since forever, the bones and homes of reality and dreams. Together we have been the matter of the earth. We have been the ones to draw from the ethers the unimaginable, to clearly draw it with our imaginings ,and then *to make it so!*

We are cosmic dust resurrected from will and power into bodies that stand in the earth, in the skies, and ever in glory. Welcome to our grand heritage. Being solid has not meant that we are not composed of chimes and chants and fair thoughts. It means we have focused these to become the art forms of the ethers. We are the sculptures of lifeforce and we have chosen to be all of these things and more.

Listen my friends, do you know the future? It is the choice to be more. We may carry these bodies into sunlight and starlight and create even newer bodies. Vehicles of our spirit ask for our conscious creating. This is the Gabriel's Dawn. While we may have fears of entering this doorway so clearly, so absolutely willfully, we enter it. What we find is the magnificence of creation stretched before us, fresh from our own fingertips. It all condenses to now. It all focuses to this choice.

I choose passing through the doorway. I choose to say aloud, "I am passing through the doorway." I am the Gabriel's Dawn and I declare this with full being to all beings. I know my freedom in this. I harbor no pride, no separation. I am crystallized in a single freedom. I bring my full breath and depth to all. I befriend any who join me and love all who don't. All that matters or manifests or creates is free. Freedom.

There. My spark of consciousness has traversed this singular doorway of choice. In doing so I treasure a piece of every consciousness inside of me and it also passes through. Do you celebrate it? Do you hear the echo of it in your cells? Whenever one of us chooses the freedom, the complete freedom we are in any now, that gift transcends through all energy to all life. Part of you has entered the doorway with me. But with your own free choice, you may or may not experience it directly. It is up to you.

In being absolute clarity, in honoring absolute clarity, the choice that comes back to you from my journey makes your choices clear. Will you choose this doorway? Will you claim it? Will you discover your own treasures in the passageway?

I am free from concern over your choice. I celebrate your freedom as much as my own. I feel no attachment to your moment, as I am already walking on to the next doorway. Because my essence revels in change, exploration, insistent curiosity and direct co-creation, I ask for your hand in this. I freely invite you to join me as an equal unlimited spark.

[This quartz vial wrapped in silver, holds phenacite, moldavite, and herkimer diamonds. It has asked for kornerupine to be complete and its matrix has already expanded to include it.]

## Forty

# Methusela

As we who have inhabited these last chapters have said, we have entered a new phase together. Our bond grows strong and sure. Our intent is crystalline: We choose to go forth, in, through, and beyond this book to a conscious partnering of spirit, stone, and human. Nothing is excluded, but we choose to focus on this to remember how well we complement each other.

I speak plainly. We the Moqui come because it is our turn to laugh and to draw out the lessons that said, "Serious only." Gabriel's Dawn comes to bring us ever to new adventure and to mark it in song. The Boji come to build, to wear, and to grow the new structures on the earth, of a brand new world. This epidote crystal presents us with the tools to build ourselves anew. These are only small facets of this adventure that we have already embarked upon each moment. It glows in the sun and facets again.

Since I lay at the root of the *Twintreess* and spiral within the water in their trunks and branches and leaves, I am elected to speak of this. There are new visions ascending within us. We come together for absolute healing. What we heal is the illusion of a wound. The illusion of this hurt says that we have been apart, that our souls were unfamiliar because of the intense physical learnings. Right now, we kiss those wounds and they are smooth. We heal them by saying we have never been apart. We ease the pain by declaring even louder that we are family and that we are our own new children in a new world.

Enter a peace of it now.

I give the gift of this ever-changing future dream to you, *Twintreess*, because it is not only yours. It is yours to share as you are doing so now. I see you going back to the earth. I feel you traveling inside of her, by night, and by sacred fires. You will rise by day with rocks and stones and crystalline bodies. These bodies enter your own. From there you travel the stars and the galactic story-tellers who know you so well. But that is another story in another place.....

Meanwhile you dance upon the earth choosing to know her depths and inviting her winds to your breath, her fires to your chakras, her oceans to your blood, and her bones to your bodies. From this, you will build new structures. You will design, from her elements, temples where all beings, human and otherwise, will gather (truthfully, they already gather there) to sing and to howl in primal affection. These structures open themselves to gatherings of spirit and whole healing. The memories in those walls are of the future coming to pass. The ancient meets the next age in those doorways.

I mean this literally. Build the new houses with the guidance of all your families. They also wish to find new homes. The family has gathered together again. As you travel the earth (and other dimensions simultaneously) you will touch, one by one, other humans. They will recognize you. They will shout, they will smile. Some will cry. All choose perfectly. The common point will be: All will awaken clearly. As they recognize you, they recognize themselves. They exalt their own beings. They know the time of the free family has arrived. We each spring from the same circle and bring to it, our single perfect unique point of light.

In your meetings, I and the stone beings, we visit freely. For myself, I ask you to transmit my words as I translate easily through your fingers, your eyes, and your smiles. In giving my messages, our cells will renew. We will place ourselves as free children upon the earth. Those who hear my words, can share them. Their love grows as they are passed on and on. New meanings will ever arise from them.

*Twintreess*, I offer my body. If you listen, you hear other offers. Carry me with you. I want to know the palms of many humans. I want to feel their lifelines. Use me to affirm the healing in the auras of the humans who come. Spiral me around their bodies at their free souls' request. I will release the need to struggle. I will highlight and honor the abundance of the human-crystal joining.

Let me translate further. You who walk into

the Aquarian Age, your physical bodies evolve into crystalline vehicles. This is your genetic gift from the earth. I can point out to you where and how your new body flowers. Rub me over your human flesh and I hear the fuel that your crystalline bodies request. I am so practiced at this type of listening. It is my heavenly gift upon the earth. It is my piece to give. It is my soul's shining. It is my laugh at the last gasp. It is my clarity at pain's clouds. It is me and I give it to you.

Let me place my gift into easy tools. What follows are holy practices. Put them in your life. Wear them until you know them. Let them design you. From there you will re-design them. This, of course, is co-creation.

Blessings. Welcome. Love.

RITUAL ONE: Sit upon the earth. Let your spine be a mountain, firm and deeply comfortable. Breathe and allow the passage of energy from above and below to travel through you. When the energy soars easily with each breath, you are at one. Circle your body with the Moqui (in form or in thought). Now breathe. Fully stretch your awareness through your breath. Do not control it in pattern, or in size, or in shape. As each breath leaves you, it forms its own artwork and sign. Breathe and see the creations form and evaporate. Create and release. You are housed in your own cosmic reality. As you breathe, you are in union with those who used to place Moquis upon the earth as models of the earth itself and as models of the whole healed world. There. You have struck our purpose and sparked it in love. The circle around you is an ancient council and a new one.

Let us merge. Receive. With each breath, receive the messages we have for you. Find the words that have your name upon them and smile. They are translated into your cells in any manner you wish. Before you leave the circle, breathe in all and release all. Breathe in all and release all. Walk in and out of this circle in great sacredness. You have just claimed a spot upon the earth for an unconditionally loving reality. The consciousness thanks you. Do this as often as you wish.

<u>RITUAL TWO</u>: Lay down upon the earth. Choose the times of new light. Dawn. Dusk. Full moon. Spread your feet slightly apart, your arms are shoulder height and stretched from your body. Place your Moquis (again, in form or in essence) in your hands, by your feet, and one in the center of your body. Surround yourself in silence. Let every sound and awareness trickle through you and heighten your listening. You breathe complete awareness. Your heart opens. You breathe as a stone in the earth that is arising. There is nothing that you need do but be quietly ready. Then choose to be quietly ready in the next moment and the next and the next. This is the story-teller's position. We will bring you the grand tales of inside the earth to tell of on the surface. Listen. We tell them in bits and songs. Sometimes we just smile in your breath. That is a very grand story indeed. Do not be concerned. However we speak to you will be the story that is for you. Witness it with your spirit and it grows louder each time you enter this position. When you are overbrimming, give them away like tears and chuckles.

## Forty One
# Thompsonite

[Thompsonite is found (as far as we know) only in one particular place on the north shore of Lake Superior in Minnesota. It is highly valued there and looks agatized and much different than that, also. This stone has many eyes and some wonderful green among its creams and reds.]

Hello.

If you have not done so already, create a ritual for our meeting. There have been some suggested in previous writings. Or, if you prefer, cast out your breath around you in all directions. See it, hear it, feel it, extend itself infinitely. If you find yourself distracted while reading this, focus on a piece of your breath. Stretch it into eternity. I join you there.

I am a Thompsonite and I am also the closing story of this book. I point the way to the next circle and the next story and I welcome it all. For now, we are breathing an ending. Let us feel that in our veins. Know the curling inward. Our regeneration is surging in us and awaiting the next exhale. I am with you at the space between the inhale and the exhale. Our meeting here is the line of dusk, the edge of day and night. What a peaceful sharpening moment this is!

All relationships formed inside of this now or inside this book leave us. We feel those other beings go as we exhale completely. There are new intimacies with each other and with new others already forming, but we stop in this moment and we BE. We simply BE the end, the pause in eternity, that is ever changing.

I invite you to huddle in closer to the death that is in these last pages. I know that many of you leave before you can feel a death. Fear asks you to rise out of your body so that you will not sense its fullness. When you comply with this the births are also muted. To always face the dawn and the new arising, means that your back is at the sunset. You are brave, you are wonderful enough to know *all* points in between because your journey on this earth is the sunrise, the sunset, and all points in between.

Come a little closer to me, brothers and sisters. We touch a forever truth here. All things end and begin and be. These points of life are not separate. They grasp each other in complete love. They envelop their selves so absolutely. They exist as one. You feel me right now. You feel these closing words and you feel my opening palms to reacquaint you and to welcome you again. Is this confusing? Can hello and good bye be the same as, I AM?

Ultimately, I am most practical. I practice life and death until it knows me. Perhaps it is an endless joke, yet I love it unconditionally. Spread out your hands. Close your eyes inward. We add to our first ritual. As you breathe, and see their tendrils, lift off into space. Now, see them clearly. Burrow them into you; they search every direction of you. (It is just as infinite as the space beyond, that you cannot see, but acknowledge with your breath). Whenever you wish, I will take your hand and breathe with you. Simply ask. Continue the inner and outer breaths. Launch them past time. Explode them past understanding. Laugh them through all. Your inhales and exhales allow grandness and quietness. They filter through your expectations and dust them to the earth. If you choose me as a friend then I am a smile at your expectations' scatterings. If you choose me as an enemy then I am the smile at your expectations' scatterings. Of course, you choose. Again, in me, I find no separation between those smiles, happy, sad, birthing, or dying. Again, here is my open palm.....

This page holds us in a remarkable embrace. It breathes us freely therefore it is the wind of change. Can you see this? My body is all eyes so I give you all my vision. This page is a page from the book of earth's life. All of your names are inscribed. Symbols of your passage rest there. This moment, this page, this breath, finds us in a full blown initiation. The doorway now marks the choice. Life. Death. All.

Remember, your vision extends as far as your breath and your choices are free, so if you do not find the option you wish, then pass through the doorway and inscribe it inside. Fellow earth-beings, we poise ourself at the dusk. As we slip from the light we have known into the darkness unknown, will we remember that life ever passes through death? Death caresses life until it is most dear.

This reigns as our pointed hour upon the earth. If you see with your breath and listen with your heart you also are a guardian of the initiation. Arise, expand your being in all directions. Arise within, expand yourself in all directions. As the outer and the inner co-mingle, so too does life and death. So too does right and wrong. So too does initiation and peace. Open your eyes with your heart. Fill them with your breath. Initiation is a gift that cleanses you, that hones you to a single point of all things. Touch it as if you knew it. Caress it as if it were you. Know it until your questions shatter.

I am with you, oh, I am with you. I even journey through the time that you have created,the initiations that you have given to me, so that I might say, "I am eternity with you." If you recognize me now it is that I have always been with you because you have asked for me forever. I tell you this rite of passage in the earth, in us, is the same. It lives the same. It dies the same. It is one with all the other initiations. You are as supported before them as you are, afterwards, when you can remember them.

Be fresh eyes, right now! Read like a child, dead and reborn every second. That is the blessing you and I extend across the doorway to each other.

It is all momentous, isn't it!

So, here we are resting in what appears to be the end of these relationships and sometimes even the end of the earth. How will you mark this upon the doorway? Initiation gives you a single moment to rise to greatness. You are this already. When the air around the earth chokes and gasps, you breathe outwardly from your precious within. Breathe with the earth. Breathe with the children. Breathe in the children. It is a birthing in the death.

Many symbols of past initiations reside all around you. Beings from other stars come to speak. You feel the earth and you feel inside the earth as never before. Your destiny intertwines with all life. Yes. When the trees die in great numbers, sweep the feeling of that into your heart and open it more. Weep so fully that you water the earth. Make way for the new seeds. Breathe like a child. Know the ending so that the beginning surprises you. The newness comes to you now. Make way for what has been, what will be, in what is.

I have an epilogue.

1996 lays its mantle upon you impressively. It seems that there is so much to do. You count wrongs to be righted and fill wounds to be healed. Blessings for the doing. The Being is eternal. It shines upon you and through all distances. In this light you can never be away. (And lost, is impossible.)

I believe in my own visions that you are standing erect to the stars. You have voted for this time to be a conscious choosing of your divine birthright which I see as BEING! You are the power, you are the light, the dark. You are the human. You are the stone. You are the Thompsonite. I know this because I feel you wearing my eyes.

Of course you give portent to this era..... You are celestial earth guardians. You have come here to tell all others this even though you know fear quite intimately. You come, to now, to resurrect your truth in words and in all doing.

Of course.

My mission, if I could call it that, complements yours. They lay side by side like easy love. So I have no answers or particular guidance because I am being with you. My gift is the vision that looks through all. If you find newness in this, absorb it. After all, it is ours. Look upon the earth. She is your blessing. She is all opportunities to accept, right now. She is every dimension. If you wish to give and share a piece of this, do so. It is free. I laugh and tell you the gift cannot be forced upon another. I laugh because I know some of you must try regardless.

To me, a guardian of these initiation times, means, not to protect from wrong or dark or death, it means to guard your truth in a reality of perfection. In that it is never truly threatened, so as a guardian you take on the task of simply speaking all of your truth. Speak every piece of it now! Speak each new piece as you explore it. Speak each one as it does. Proclaim them. Then speak them again as they create a new world.

There is no need, sweet guardians, to judge the next world. Draw it from the lines of eternity. They pass through you in each moment, timelessly precious. We live in these initiations to release expectation and limits. You are children at that death. Cry for what you have known. Weave the tears and the anger through you. Once outside of your body they are dust in the earth. Once outside of your beliefs you are free!

Arise guardians. Pull your truth from your ethers. Give it voice. Once outside of your body it is free. We are all the initiations.

As for the *Twintreess*, you and time create a space to travel. Your bodies speak of walking upon the earth, and there are oceans, waterfalls, other continents, already breathing you. The rhythms of the earth's organs pulse with you. Her lungs breathe with you and her heart bleeds into you. You feel called to lay with her, to be with her, to write of wholeness. It is unbelievable to some. It is your truth to give. Give till you have no more and you are free.

These words and all their children-words soar around and through this planet. They breathe in the wholes. They gasp, and still, they choose to go on. None of this flatters you. It is the truth of all dimensions honed to a single point. It sharpens your challenges and your ease. In that sharpening you find new vision that stalks the other dreams. Abundance surely follows.

A new home comes to you. The choice is yours. Many others also ask you to design and to build the houses that stand upon the earth, in happy initiation. These structures speak of truth, always known in the unknown.

In this, the Moqui asked to be a particular guardian. I see this clearly and my vision is there for the asking, not my telling. Decide... as you need and desire to do so.

The new buildings (and only some of them are literal buildings, others are works of art and healing) spring from the trees within you. What gifts arise from the branches, as you release the questions and the needs! Build simply like a child. No foreknowledge of a storm truly protects you. Build. I have seen your interdimensional cities and many, many join you. They do not require these structures but honor them as the ritual that speaks your newly joined languages of all life forms.

Blessings.

<u>To Brad and Anna</u>*: What amazing times! Your truth weaves through words and comes out the other end to the beginning. Isn't this what a channel is? Now, in these moments of absolute portent and omens, you wear the truth that you speak. You model the bear, the fish, the crab, the warrior, the dog, the aliens, the mountains, the flowers, and most of all now, fear (the earth.)

*Host/publishers/friends of these stories.

Welcome. The challenge pushing through your veins clears the inner earth, spills over the edges. It is time to celebrate that it is so easy, that it is your moment, even as you believe that you are below the challenge and less than your choices. You support the new homes and the new altars. They arise from your creations. They touch the stars and circle back to the earth. That is the dawning and giving of hope. Those who can freely go to the other planets and choose to be here, extend all blessings and prosperity to those who are here and have never dreamt of anywhere else.

This is your choice. You are clothing yourself in it consciously. It is indeed wondrously ominous. Write that ending and beginning as you choose.

For Alison and Zoe (children of TreeHouse Press): Welcome new guardians. You can choose to be children forever. This does not mean that you are always going to be small and always going to be shaped. It means you are ever free. Be kind. Your freedom shapes those around you. Remember to smile. Many believe the initiation is very hard, very serious. Perhaps you will know some of this soon and perhaps you will forget it again.

Through your choice of birth, you have chosen to be the earth's birth. Such visions come in that exact moment of creation. That awaits outside of you yet, and that awaits you, inside of you. No wisdom do I give you. You are free.

The end.

# Acknowledgements

We would like to acknowledge here the gifts of sharing that some special human friends gave us in allowing us to include in this book the stories of some of their special stones and to allow us to keep those stones with us over a certain period of time/ timelessness.

Thank you Debra Kay and James for sharing the phantom elestial and the 13-sided Vogel crystal.
Thank you Teresa for listening and sharing your necklace of dioptase.
Thank you Don for sharing the fossilized whale tooth.
Thank you to the guys who threw the rock through our truck's window.
And again, a special thanks to Karen, the Boji mother, for the gift of the two special Boji, and for introducing us to the Moqui stones.

Blessings to you all for being in our lives. We love you.

# Join Us

*Thank you for allowing The Heart of Matter into your life. We feel the immensity of the joining of these stone stories with your humanity (and ours) strongly. If you would like to go further down this same path and hear the story of your favorite or personal or significant stone, call or write us. We can tune into the vibration of your stone wherever it is and wherever we are and can give you its story. We feel certain stones come into our lives for very specific reasons. It is very powerful to hear them speak for themselves why they have chosen their relationship with you.*

How it works: Call or write us to set up an appointment for us to speak with your stone. We need only hear its description from you or see its picture. We will write down your stone's story and send it back to you immediately.

The Cost: $44.00 prepaid. (Price is subject to change without notice.)

*Twintreess*
5738 E. Holmes St.
Tucson, AZ 85711 USA
1-800-585-9389

More Books by *Twintreess*:

*Naturespeak*
*Etheric Songs from the Children of Earth*
*Windows on other Worlds*
*Nurturance of the Soul into Forever:*
*Ad/Rift in A/Maze*
*Meditations on Regeneration*

And:
*The Rituals of Manifestation Deck*

To order, to receive a catalog of all of our products and services, and/or get on our mailing list, simply call TreeHousePress @ 1-800-585-9389.